WHO ARE YOU GOING TO CALL THIS TIME?

"Look, lady," said the cop into the phone. "Of course there are dead people there. It's a cemetery. . . . What? . . . They were asking you for *directions*?"

"Was this a big dinosaur or a little dinosaur?" another cop asked. "Oh, just a skeleton, huh? Heading toward Central Park?"

Another detective sighed and shook his head. "Wait a second. You say the park bench was chasing you? You mean someone was chasing you in the park, don't you? . . . No, the bench itself was galloping after you. I see . . ."

He called to his lieutenant. "Sir, I think you better talk to this guy."

The lieutenant faced the cop. "I have problems of my own."

"What's up?"

"It's some dock supervisor down at Pier Thirty-four on the Hudson. The guy's going nuts!"

"What's the problem?"

"He says the *Titanic*

GHOSTBUSTERS II

A NOVEL BY
Ed Naha
BASED ON A MOTION PICTURE WRITTEN BY
Harold Ramis AND Dan Aykroyd

BASED ON THE CHARACTERS CREATED BY
Dan Aykroyd AND Harold Ramis

An Ivan Reitman Film
STARRING
Bill Murray, Dan Aykroyd, Sigourney Weaver, Harold Ramis, Rick Moranis

CORGI BOOKS

GHOSTBUSTERS II
A CORGI BOOK 0 552 13575 5

First published in USA by Dell Publishing, a division of the Bantam Doubleday Dell Publishing Group, Inc.

First publication in Great Britain

PRINTING HISTORY
Corgi edition published 1989

Corgi Books are published by Transworld Publishers Ltd., 61–63 Uxbridge Road, Ealing, London W5 5SA, in Australia by Transworld Publishers (Australia) Pty. Ltd., 15–23 Helles Avenue, Moorebank, NSW 2170, and in New Zealand by Transworld Publishers (N.Z.) Ltd., Cnr. Moselle and Waipareira Avenues, Henderson, Auckland.

Printed and bound in Great Britain by
Cox & Wyman Ltd., Reading, Berks.

For Suzanne,
Happy 1st

I

"The universe is full of magical things patiently waiting for our wits to grow sharper."

—EDEN PHILLPOTTS

•

"Spengler, are you serious about actually catching a ghost?"

—DR. PETER VENKMAN

1

A bright winter sun blazed down onto the streets of Manhattan as Dana Barrett struggled with two sagging bags of groceries while at the same time pushing a baby carriage.

Long-armed and lithe in figure, Dana was able to balance the bags in her arms while still maneuvering the carriage in a straight line.

Pausing for a moment, she took a deep breath of crisp air. She loved New York. It was the city's air of excitement, of *life* that appealed to her. As she continued walking, she thought about how her life had changed in the last four years. How many women could say that they'd been a struggling cellist, been attacked by a devilishly possessed chair, been transformed into an ancient demon, and, finally, become a mother of a bright-eyed baby named Oscar—all in the few years since she'd moved to the Big Apple?

Not many, she figured. At least not many who were allowed to roam the streets without a straitjacket.

Dana wheeled her baby up to the front of her

building on East Seventy-seventh Street. At curbside, a car was being hoisted up by a city tow truck while the driver screamed, red-faced, at the parking-enforcement officer. The man was threatening to do something to the cop that dogs usually reserved for hydrants.

Dana clutched the grocery bags, trying desperately to dig her keys out of her purse.

Glancing over her shoulder, she noticed that Frank, her building's superintendent, was leaning against a wall, pretending not to notice Dana's dilemma. Typical, she thought. Frank was the sort of fellow who lived in the future. If something needed repairing, he'd put it off until tomorrow, or next week, or, if it was really important, next month.

Dana turned and smiled sweetly at Frank. "Frank, do you think you could give me a hand with these bags?"

The unshaven, middle-aged man shrugged. "I'm not a doorman, Miss Barrett. I'm a building superintendent."

Dana resisted the temptation to hurl a few choice canned goods at Frank's head. "You're also a human being, Frank."

Frank considered this point. Yup, he was. Reluctantly he walked toward Dana. "Okay. Okay. It's not my job, but what the heck. I'll do you a big favor." With a grunt he took the sagging grocery bags out of Dana's arms.

"Thank you, Frank, you're a prince."

"Better." Frank grinned. "I'm a *super*."

Dana set the wheel brakes on the baby carriage and rummaged through her purse. "I'll get the hang of all this eventually," she muttered.

Frank leaned over the baby buggy and began making funny faces at little Oscar. "Hiya, Oscar. What do you say, slugger?"

Oscar regarded the crazy person above him with a great deal of disinterest. The baby couldn't figure out why most adults acted goofy when they were around him. Little Oscar sighed and concentrated on his pacifier.

Frank didn't notice. "That's a good-looking kid you got there, Ms. Barrett."

Dana found her keys at the very bottom of her purse. Typical. "Thank you, Frank."

Dana turned to her superintendent. "Oh, and are you ever going to fix the radiator in my bedroom? I asked you last week."

Frank blinked in astonishment. "Didn't I do it?"

Dana flashed him a patented grin. "No, you didn't."

"Okay," Frank said, still holding the soggy bags. "That's no problem."

"That's exactly what you said last week."

Frank thought hard about this. "Phew! Déjà vu."

While Dana and Frank stared at each other, little Oscar's baby carriage began to shake and rock, as if being cradled by unseen hands.

The wheel brakes unlocked themselves.

Dana, still smiling stoically at Frank, reached for Oscar's carriage. "You wouldn't mind carrying those bags upstairs, would you, Frank?"

"Well . . . actually . . ." Frank began.

As Dana extended her hand for the carriage, the carriage moved forward, just out of her reach. Dana glanced at the carriage suspiciously, as it came to a stop two feet before her.

She walked over to the buggy and tried to grab it again. The buggy shook and shot out of Dana's reach. This time it didn't rumble to a halt. It rolled merrily down the block, little Oscar inside, clapping and chirping with glee. This was *fast*. This was *fun*.

Dana fought back the urge to emit a shriek. She continued to plunge forward through the crowds of pedestrians, shambling about the streets of Manhattan.

Behind her, a befuddled Frank still stood, holding the leaking grocery bags. "Uh . . ." he considered. "Ms. Barrett? What should I do with these bags?"

Dana decided not to tell him what to do with the bags. She sprinted after the runaway carriage.

Little Oscar raised a tiny fist as his baby buggy zoomed down the Manhattan street.

The baby giggled happily, watching the Upper East Side zip by.

Dana jogged, awestruck, after the baby carriage.

She shouted to everybody, *any*body, for help. "Please," she screamed. "Please help my baby! Please help him!"

Several passersby tried to reach out and stop the runaway buggy. Every time they did so, the carriage deftly swerved out of the way, leaving the would-be rescuers stunned in its wake.

Little Oscar continued to giggle as the baby carriage picked up speed and zigzagged like an Indy 500 race car.

Dana continued to gallop forward. The baby buggy seemed to have a life of its own. Dana yelled for help. One burly man tried to tackle the baby carriage and found himself being lifted and thrown *over* it by some unseen force.

In the speeding baby buggy, baby Oscar clapped his hands with glee. *Zoooooom*, he managed to gurgle. *Zooooooom.*

The buggy tilted and whirled past everyone on the street.

The buggy headed for a crosswalk.

Cars, trucks, and buses zipped through the congested intersection ahead.

Dana watched in horror as a city bus glided across Seventy-seventh Street. Effortlessly the baby buggy sailed over the curb and into the intersection.

The carriage was speeding toward the front of the bus.

Dana took a deep breath and, tilting her head down, sent her long legs pumping toward the intersection like an Olympic sprinter.

Inside, baby Oscar watched in fascination as the large vehicle zeroed in on the buggy.

The bus driver, spotting the runaway carriage, twisted the steering wheel before him frantically.

The baby carriage came to a dead stop in the middle of the street.

The bus driver, still pawing the wheel, managed to send the vehicle swerving around little Oscar, missing him by inches.

Car horns blared and brakes screeched as Dana leapt into the busy intersection, quickly snatching Oscar out of the buggy.

She held the baby tightly in her arms and stared at the baby carriage.

The carriage seemed normal—now.

It stood in the center of the intersection, immobile.

To the casual passerby it appeared to be just another carriage.

Dana backed away from the buggy, Oscar in her arms.

She knew *better*.

2

A slim, elegant 1959 ambulance tooled up Broadway on the Upper West Side of Manhattan. On the side of the vehicle was painted a portrait of a ghost, surrounded by a red circle with a crimson slash drawn through it. "No Ghosts."

The vehicle bore the license plate ECTO-1 and was, in fact, the Ghostbusters' emergency vehicle.

Inside Ecto-1, a very tired Ray Stantz helmed the steering wheel while a very bored Winston Zeddemore rode shotgun. Both wore their official Ghostbusters jumpsuits, and both were ready for trouble.

Stantz guided the vehicle around potholes. A tall, baby-faced man with a haircut that could only be described as New Wave groundhog, Stantz rubbed his eyes occasionally, trying to get the red out.

As a light turned green ahead, he gave Ecto-1 the gas. The car produced a sound that sounded like a yak in a blender.

Big, burly, and black, Winston Zeddemore slid

deeper into his seat. He was beginning to hate this work. A lot.

"How many did she say there were?" Winston asked.

Stantz peered into the bus-fume-laced street before him. "Fourteen of them," he said in a monotone. "About three and a half to four feet high."

Winston heaved a sigh. "I don't think I can take this anymore, man. All the crying and the biting! The screaming and the fighting! It's starting to get to me, Ray."

Stantz nodded grimly. "I know it's rough, Winston, but somebody's got to do it. People are counting on us. Who else are they going to call . . . *Bozo the clown*?"

A thin smile played across Stantz's lips. "I . . . don't . . . think . . . so."

Stantz guided the car into a parking space before a carefully restored old brownstone. Gritting his teeth, he marched out of Ecto-1 and strode to the back of the refurbished ambulance. He popped open the back hatch and produced two large, bulky proton packs attached to neutrona wands—ghostbusting guns hooked up to power-generating backpacks.

Winston and Stantz, grim-faced, shouldered their weapons in place and marched up to the building, their eyes darting this way and that.

They stopped before the front door. Stantz pressed a buzzer. "Who is it?" a female voice squawked over the intercom. "Ghostbusters," Stantz said coolly. "We have a job to do here."

The woman sighed over the intercom. In the background could be heard wailing and screeching voices.

"I'll say," the woman said. "Come on in. It's Apartment 1-B."

Stantz and Winston exchanged determined looks as

they entered the building and walked down a dimly lit, cavernous hallway, proton packs strapped firmly in place.

"This could be a rough one," Stantz stated.

"I know it," Winston agreed. "I heard."

They paused before the door.

"This is it," Stantz declared.

Winston nodded. "This is it."

Stantz made a move to reach for the knocker on the door. Before he had a chance to grasp it, the door was flung open. A birdlike woman with blue-gray hair and what appeared to be makeup left over from an Earl Scheib paint job greeted them nervously.

"They're in the back!" she gasped. "I hope you can handle them. It's been like a nightmare!"

Stantz and Winston exchanged knowing glances. Winston nodded and his jaw tightened. "We'll do our best, ma'am."

"Oh, thank you," the woman gushed. "They're right in here."

The tiny woman led the two Ghostbusters through an expensively furnished home. She stopped in front of a pair of opened French doors, leading into a vast living room.

Ray Stantz and Winston paused before the door. They carefully adjusted their equipment.

"Ready?" Stantz asked, sweat trickling down his forehead.

"I'm ready," Winston declared, straightening himself up to his full six-feet-plus height.

"Let's *do* it!" Stantz whispered.

The two men strode past the French doors and marched into the living room.

"Oh, my God!" Winston said.

"It's worse than I thought!" Stantz gulped.

Over a dozen children—short, birthday-cake-stained, and all between the ages of seven and ten—descended upon the two helpless men.

"Ghostbusters!" they screeched.

"Yeah!" others shouted.

Stantz glanced around the room. Tables were set with party favors, dripping with left-over ice cream and birthday cake. The place was scattered with discarded toys and games. Several exhausted parents were strewn across sofas. They glanced at Stantz and Winston as they entered the room. They made eye contact. Their eyes said, "Thank you, thank you, thank you."

Winston winked at the parents and faced the horde of ice-cream- and cake-stained short people before him. "How you doin', kids?" he asked.

A freckle-faced kid with a big belly glared at Winston. "I thought we were having He-Man."

To stress the point, the mean little kid brought his right leg way back and kicked Stantz in the shin. Stantz smiled and, after making sure no parents were watching, reached down and grabbed the kid by the front of his shirt. He smiled at the little boy. "I'll be watching you," he growled. "Remember that."

He dropped the kid back onto the floor and turned to Winston with a wink. "Song?"

Winston reached into his utility belt and switched on a tiny tape recorder, which began belting out the Ghostbusters' theme song. Stantz and Winston began gyrating, singing, and bopping to the music.

Who you gonna call?" they crooned.

"He-Man," the kids replied.

Stantz and Winston glanced at each other, not breaking stride.

"It's gonna be one of those gigs," Winston hissed.

"Keep singing, we need the money," Stantz said, breaking out into the Twist.

A small eternity later, Stantz found himself surrounded by drippy-nosed children. He was trying to keep them amused by recounting the Ghostbusters' finest hour. "So," he continued, "we get up to the very top of the building, and yep, sure enough, there was a huge staircase with those two nasty terror dogs I told you about. And guess what?"

"They were guarding the entrance," the wise-guy kid said with a sigh.

Stantz tried not to strangle the little beastie. "Exactly." He smiled. "They were guarding the entrance. Well, at this point I had to take command, so I turned to the boys and I said, 'Okay, 'Busters, this is it. Fire up your throwers and let's toast that sucker!'"

The mean little kid wasn't impressed. "My dad says you're full of crap."

Stantz's eyes almost left his head. "Well, a lot of people have trouble believing in the paranormal," he offered.

"Naah," the kid continued, "that's not it. He says you're full of crap and that's why you went out of business."

Stantz flashed a smile of the sort usually used by bodybuilders hiding a groin injury. "He does, eh? I see."

Stantz snapped his fingers, getting up from the crowd of children. "Hey! How about some science? Did you ever see a hard-boiled egg get sucked through the mouth of a Coke bottle?"

The kids nodded in unison. "Yeah," they said.

"A lot," the mean little kid added.

Winston sat in a corner and shook his head. "Oh, man," he said, then sighed.

After Stantz had pummeled every Mr. Wizard trick

into the carpet, the weary Ghostbusters packed up their gear and trudged out of the building.

Stantz popped open Ecto-1's back hatch and tossed his equipment inside. Winston neatly knuckle-balled his into the auto.

"That's it, Ray," he swore. "I've had it. No more parties. I'm tired of taking abuse from overprivileged nine-year-olds."

"Come on, Winston," Stantz wheedled, trying to look on the bright side of things. "We can't quit now. The holidays are coming up! It's our best season!"

The two men got into the car. Stantz attempted to get Ecto-1 moving. He cranked the ignition key. The car made a sound that resembled an elephant in heat. The engine refused to turn over. Winston gazed out of the windshield at nothing in particular.

"Give it up, Ray. You're living in the past. Ghostbusters doesn't exist anymore. In a year these kids won't even remember who we are."

Stantz plowed a hand through his groundhog hairdo before cranking the engine again. *Snork!* the engine declared before dying. "Ungrateful little yuppie larvae," Stantz muttered. "After all we did for this city!"

Winston offered a dry cackle. "Yeah, what did we do, Ray? The last real job we had, we bubbled up a hundred-foot marshmallow man and blew the top three floors off an uptown high rise."

A dreamy smile played across Stantz's face. "Yeah, but what a *ride*. You can't make a hamburger without chopping up a cow."

Stantz turned the ignition key again. Ecto-1's engine roared to life. Then it began to grind its gears. Then, apparently, it began playing a game of last tag with itself. Stantz couldn't believe his ears as, *clunkity-clunk-clunk*, the engine began tossing off twisted little bits of itself onto the street beneath it. A massive cloud of black smoke mushroomed from the back of the car. Stantz gaped at the dashboard as every "danger" indicator lit up and Ecto-1 sputtered, shuddered, spat, and died.

Winston gave him an I-told-you-so look.

Ray Stantz considered the situation and reacted in an adult manner. He began to bang his forehead onto the steering wheel.

"You're going to hurt yourself, Ray," Winston offered.

"I know," Stantz said, slamming his forehead, again and again, onto the wheel.

"Want me to call Triple A?" Winston asked.

"Either that or a brain surgeon," Stantz replied.

Winston eased himself out of Ecto-1. "I'll see who answers first."

3

Legend has it that even as a child, Peter Venkman was incapable of a sincere smile. The farthest he could go was a heartfelt smirk. In high school he was voted Most Likely to Become a Used-car Salesman or a Game-show Host. Venkman never cared. He knew he had it within himself to achieve *greatness*. And if he didn't find it within himself, he knew he could probably pick it up somewhere at a discount.

He'd been great once. A bona fide Ghostbuster.

Now, the fellow with the twenty-four-hour smirk, the cocky attitude, and hair that looked like it had been dried by a Mixmaster sat in the tiny TV studio given to him by WKRR, Channel 10, in New York.

He sat passively in his host's seat, gazing out on an audience filled with polyester leisure suits and dresses that resembled designs lifted from Omar the tent maker.

Synthesized Muzak began to play in the background.

He glanced at the TV monitor to the right of the camera as the title *World of the Psychic with Dr. Peter*

Venkman materialized against a background that looked like swirling phlegm.

Venkman screwed on his best grin (which operated at a forty-five-degree angle) and pushed his voice up to gracious-huckster volume. He was suave. He was engaging. He was the people's friend. He would do anything to pay the rent.

"Hi," he said breathlessly to both the camera and the adoring audience. "We're back to the *World of the Psychic.* I'm Peter Venkman."

He glanced at his two guests: a frail man who resembled Boris Karloff after a bad day in the lab and a rotund woman who bore more than a passing resemblance to Lou Costello in drag.

"I'm chatting with my guest—author, lecturer, and of course, psychic, Milton Anglund."

He faced the dour man and cocked his head to one side in a Cary Grant kind of way. "Milt, your new book is called *The End of the World.* Isn't that kind of like writing about gum disease? Yes, it could happen, but do you think anybody wants to read a book about it?"

The dour man shrugged. "Well, I think it's important for people to know that the world is in danger."

Venkman nodded. "Okay, so you can tell us when it's going to happen or do we have to buy the book?"

Milton puffed up his sparrowlike chest. "I predict that the world will end at the stroke of midnight on New Year's Eve."

Venkman rolled his eyes. "This year? That's cutting it a little close, isn't it? I mean, from a sales point of view, the book just came out, right? So you're not even looking at the paperback release for maybe a year. And it's going to be at least another year after that if the thing has movie-of-the-week or miniseries potential. You would have been better off predicting 1992 or even '94 just to play it safe."

Milton was not amused. "This is not just some money-making scheme! I didn't just make up the date. I have a strong psychic belief that the world will end on New Year's Eve!"

Venkman raised his palms. "Whoa. Okay. For your sake, I hope you're right. But I think my other guest may disagree with you. Elaine, you had another date in mind, right?"

The heavily made-up woman from New Jersey nodded her head. "According to my sources, the world will end on February fourteenth, in the year 2016."

Venkman winked at her. "Valentine's Day? That's got to be a bummer. Where did you get that date, Elaine?"

Elaine pursed her lips dramatically. "I received this information from an alien. I was at the Paramus Holiday Inn. I was having a drink in the bar when he approached me and started talking. Then he must have used some sort of ray or a mind-control device, because he made me follow him to his room and that's where he told me about the end of the world."

Venkman grinned as he felt a good number of his brain cells check out. "Your alien had a room at the Holiday Inn?"

Elaine pondered this. "It may have been a room on the spacecraft made up to *look* like a room in the Holiday Inn."

Venkman gazed at the woman. He was losing feeling in his feet. "No, you can't be *sure*," he said with a nod. "And I think that's the whole problem with aliens. You just can't trust them. Oh, sure, you may get some nice ones occasionally, like Starman or E.T., but most of them turn out to be some kind of lizard. Anyway, we're just about out of time."

Venkman faced the camera, mentally nodding out. "Next week on *World of the Psychic* . . . Bigfoot: is he real or just a lumberjack from a broken home?"

He smiled at the camera. "Until then, this is Peter Venkman . . . good night."

After the show he cornered his producer, Norman, in the hall. Norman looked a little like Timmy from the old *Lassie* show but was slightly better dressed.

"Where do you find these people, *Normie*?" Venkman asked. "I thought we were having the telekinetic guy who bends the spoons?"

Norman was embarrassed. "A lot of the better psychics won't come onto your show, Dr. Venkman. They think you're too skeptical."

"Me?" Venkman said, astonished. "Skeptical? Norman, I'm a pushover. I think professional wrestling is real!"

Venkman looked up. There was a commotion brewing from the studio next door. Several plainclothes policemen strode out of two swinging doors, followed by a small army of men in suits, with serious expressions.

"What's all this?" Venkman asked Norman.

"They just interviewed the mayor on *Cityline*," Norman replied.

"The Mayor of New York City!" Venkman exclaimed. "Why, he's an old friend of mine."

Venkman ran down the corridor as the mayor and his top aide—a mousse-laden, no-nonsense, three-piece suit named Jack Hardemeyer—emerged from the studio next door.

"Lenny!" Venkman called, waving at the mayor.

Mayor Leonard Clotch wheeled around and, spotting Venkman, wiped a trickle of sweat from his upper lip and almost ran down the hall in the opposite direction.

"Hey, Lenny!" Venkman called. "It's me! Peter Venkman."

Two plainclothes cops stopped Venkman in his tracks. Hardemeyer marched up to Venkman and, after adjusting his hair, placed a heavy hand on Venkman's chest.

"Can I help you?" He sneered.

Venkman, while appreciating the sneer, didn't like the man's attitude. "Yeah," he said, "you can get your hand off my chest."

Hardemeyer offered a serpent's smile and dropped his hand. "I'm Jack Hardemeyer. I'm the mayor's assistant. What can I do for you?"

Venkman straightened his tie. "I'm an old friend of the mayor's. I just wanted to say hello."

Hardemeyer emitted a harsh laugh. "I know who you are, Dr. Venkman. Busted any ghosts lately?"

"No," Venkman admitted. "That's what I want to talk to the mayor about. We did a little job for the city a while back and we ended up getting sued, screwed, and tattooed by desk worms like you."

Hardemeyer offered Venkman an angry stare. "Look," he replied, bristling. "You stay away from the mayor. Next fall, barring a disaster, he's going to be elected governor of this state, and the last thing we need is for him to be associated with two-bit frauds and publicity hounds like you and your friends. You read me?"

Yeah, Venkman thought to himself, and it's strictly big print.

The two plainclothes cops flanked Venkman, helping him get the point. "Okay," Venkman said smoothly.

"I get it. But I want you to tell Lenny that because of *you,* I'm not voting for him."

Hardemeyer smiled smugly and, spinning on his heels, marched off with the two plainclothes cops. Venkman watched them move out of the hallway.

Heaving a sigh, he trudged through the reception area, where a small group of his fans and possible guests were gathered.

The fans applauded him.

"No, really, you're too kind." Venkman was nearly grimacing.

One man was holding a crystal the size of a Toyota.

Another man had a small TV antenna glued to the hat he was wearing.

A fellow in full voodoo uniform sat next to the candy machine, burning incense.

A fat woman petting a hairless cat smiled up at Venkman.

Venkman smiled at them all, but at a strange angle. He was losing it. He was definitely losing it. He winked at the woman. "Nice cat. Very unusual. I had a bald collie once myself."

Venkman eased himself out the exit door and walked toward the elevator.

After thinking about it a second, he *ran.*

4

Dana Barrett walked up the stairs of the Manhattan Museum of Art, her portfolio and artist's box in her hand. She weaved her way through the crowds of tourists and visitors milling toward the museum's entrance.

Little Oscar would be safe today, she knew. She gave strict instructions to the baby-sitter not to take the boy out of the apartment.

Dana flashed her ID card at the guard at the main entrance and, ignoring his smile, walked into the back of the museum, where the large restoration studio was housed.

Since leaving her dreams of cello playing behind, Dana had earned a living restoring some of the oldest long-lost paintings of the Western world; chipping, cleaning, and urging them back into full bloom.

She stepped into the restoration studio and glanced upward with a slight shudder.

A titanic portrait of Vigo the Carpathian stared down at her. The seventeenth-century despot bore a striking resemblance to the Incredible Hulk dressed for an evening in Camelot. Vigo's dark, evil eyes seemed to leap out of the painting toward Dana.

Actually it was the artistry of a young, wiry, and decidedly quirky artist, Janosz Poha, that was bringing Vigo "to life."

Janosz was the head of the department and incredibly talented. He was also incredibly creepy to Dana's way of thinking. What he saw in the ugly painting of Vigo was beyond her.

Dana walked over to a ninteenth-century painting, this one a landscape, her mind still on little Oscar, and began to clean the years of soot and dust off its surface.

Janosz stopped working on Vigo for a moment, and staring longingly at Dana, softly padded up behind her. He looked over her shoulder and smiled. He opened his mouth and spoke, his words emerging in a thick Eastern European accent.

"Still working on the Turner?" he said casually, sounding a tad like a talking Veg-O-Matic.

"Oh?" Dana said, startled. "Oh, yes. I got in a little late this morning, Janosz. I'm sorry. I'll have it finished by the end of the day."

Janosz twisted his scarecrow face into a grin. "Take your time. The painting's been around for a hundred and fifty years. A few more hours won't matter."

Dana forced herself to emit a polite laugh. She began to work again, hoping her young boss would just go away. "You know," Janosz continued, "you are really doing very good work here. I think soon you may be ready to assist me in some of the more important restorations."

"Thank you, Janosz," Dana said, still not facing the man. "I've learned a lot here, but now that my baby's a little older, I was hoping to rejoin the orchestra."

At the mention of Dana's baby, the figure of Vigo in the painting seemed to glow slightly, its dark eyes gleaming. Slowly, deliberately, the painting turned its mighty head and gazed down at Dana.

Dana, her back toward the mural, did not notice. Neither did Janosz, who was deeply involved in gazing at Dana himself. "Oh, I'm sorry to hear that," he said. "We'll be very sorry to lose you."

Dana continued to clean her landscape. "I didn't really want to quit the orchestra in the first place," she explained. "But it's a little hard to play a cello when you're pregnant."

Janosz emitted a braying, nasal laugh. "Of course. Perhaps I could take you to lunch to celebrate your return to the Philharmonic?"

"Actually I'm not eating lunch today," Dana said, putting down her cleaning tools. "I have an appointment."

She gazed at her wristwatch. "In fact, I'd better go."

Dana replaced her tools. Janosz was clearly disturbed. "Every day I ask you to lunch, and every day you've got something else to do. Do I have bad breath or something?"

Dana smiled at him. "Something. Perhaps some other time."

Janosz brightened. "Okay. I'll take a rain check on that."

Dana walked out of the room, leaving a smiling Janosz to return to his easel. "I think she likes me." He winked at the towering painting above him.

Reaching for his small tape-player, Janosz flipped on a tape and began practicing his English phraseology as he once again resumed work on Vigo.

High above the unsuspecting Janosz, the portrait of the all-evil Vigo rolled its eyes heavenward.

Silly mortals.

5

A gaggle of Manhattan University graduate students carefully examined a small, rectangular bit of nouveau scientific gadgetry in a lab at the university's Institute for Advanced Theoretical Research while Egon Spengler, the last of the original Ghostbusters, sat at his desk listening to a thoroughly distraught Dana Barrett recount her tale of the baby buggy with a mind of its own.

Egon's face was a portrait of intense concentration, which wasn't surprising, considering that Egon had two expressions. Intense concentration and *more* intense concentration. Egon had been born to wear a lab coat. He felt out of place when not involved in some sort of experiment involving techno-wizardry.

Egon had a hawklike face and a neatly kept hairdo, separated by a pair of horn-rimmed glasses that, while out-of-date, fit his concerned face perfectly. Nothing seemed to faze earnest Egon. He had grown up idolizing two men: Albert Einstein and *Star Trek*'s Mr. Spock. Neither were known as party animals.

Dana finished her tale of roller-coaster carriage goings-on. ". . . and then the buggy just suddenly stopped dead in the middle of the street."

Egon nodded sagely. "Did anyone else see this happen?"

"Hundreds of people," Dana replied. "Believe me, I didn't imagine this."

Egon's brain was already in high gear. "I'm not saying you did. In science, we always look for the simplest explanation."

A graduate student ran up to Egon. "We're ready, Dr. Spengler."

Spengler didn't take his eyes off Dana. "We'll start with the negative calibration."

The student handed Egon the small black box. Spengler glanced at it, adjusting its controls.

"What are you working on, Egon?" Dana asked.

Egon got to his feet. "You might find this amusing," he said, attempting to smile. It hurt his face. "I'm trying to determine whether human emotional states have a measurable effect on the psychomagnetheric energy field. It's a theory Ray and I were working on when we had to dissolve Ghostbusters."

Dana didn't understand a word he was saying. "Oh, I see."

Egon led Dana to a large curtain. One of his students pulled back the drapes to reveal a large picture window. It was actually a two-way mirror looking into a small waiting room. Inside the waiting room, Dana saw a young couple apparently in the midst of a heated argument.

Egon pointed to the couple. "They think they're in here for marriage counseling. We've kept them waiting for two hours and we've been gradually increasing the temperature in the room."

He checked a heat sensor located next to the two-way glass. "It's up to ninety-five degrees at the moment. Now, one of my assistants is going to enter the room and ask them if they'd mind waiting another half hour."

He turned to Dana confidentially. "This should be good."

As Spengler, Dana, and the research team watched, one of Spengler's assistants entered the waiting room and, gesturing wildly, told the young couple about the delay. The two people leapt to their feet and began screeching at both the assistant and each other.

Spengler calmly raised the small black box and took the readings from the room.

Dana stood there, baffled.

"We'll do the happiness index next," Spengler explained.

"I-I'm sure you will," Dana said.

"As for your problem," Spengler went on, "I'd like to bring Ray in on your case, if it's all right with you."

"Okay, whatever you think," Dana answered. "But please, not Venkman!"

Spengler almost laughed out loud but caught himself in time. "Oh, no. Don't worry about *that*."

Dana attempted to look casual. "Do you, um, ever see him anymore?"

"Occasionally," Egon said.

"How is he these days?" Dana asked.

Spengler cast her a wise look. "Venkman? I think he was borderline for a while there. Then he crossed the border."

"Does he ever mention me?" Dana queried.

Spengler turned to a second pair of curtains. "No," he said with a shrug. "Not that I can recall."

He drew the drapes and peered down on a tiny little girl playing with a wonderful array of colorful toys.

Dana tried to hide her disappointment about Venkman's lack of interest in her. "Well," she said, sighing. "We didn't part on very good terms, and we sort of lost track of each other when I got married—"

One of Spengler's aides interrupted. "We're ready for the affection test."

"Good." Egon nodded. "Send in the puppy."

"I thought of calling him after my marriage ended," Dana babbled on, "but . . . anyway, I appreciate your doing this, Egon."

Egon watched as another assistant entered the playroom with an adorable cocker spaniel puppy. He gave it to the little girl. Spengler monitored her as she jumped for joy and embraced the tiny puppy affectionately.

Dana thrust a card in front of the busy Spengler's nose. "This is my address and telephone number. Will you call me?"

Spengler studied the little girl and the puppy. "Huh? Oh, certainly. Yes."

"And, Egon," Dana continued, "I'd rather you didn't mention any of this to Peter if you don't mind."

"I won't," Spengler said absentmindedly.

"Thank you," Dana said, shaking the preoccupied Spengler's hand before leaving.

Spengler watched the little girl oooh and aahh over the puppy dog.

Spengler nodded knowingly to his study team. "Now . . . let's see how she reacts when we take the puppy away."

6

Ray Stantz's Occult Bookstore sat on a small, quaint block in Greenwich Village. The window was crowded with occult artifacts and ancient books filled with arcane metaphysical lore that appealed only to the very rich, the very bored, or the very addled.

Stantz sat inside the shop on a bar stool behind the main counter while Egon Spengler waddled up and down the aisles of the tiny place, occasionally stopping to peruse a volume.

Stantz, reading glasses on, prepared a cup of herb tea for his old Ghostbuster crony while chewing on a pipe that emitted an odor reminiscent of week-old sweat socks.

The phone rang.

Stantz was amazed. A customer! Summoning up his most pleasant voice, he picked up the phone. "Ray's Occult," he said sweetly. "Yes. Uh-hmmmm. What do you need? . . . What have I got?"

Stantz took a deep breath. "I've got alchemy, astrology, apparitions, Bundu magic men, demon intercessions, UFO abductions, psychic surgery, stigmata, modern miracles, pixie sightings, golden geese, geists, ghosts. I've got it all. What is it you're looking for? Don't have any. Try the stockyards."

Stantz slammed the phone down.

"Who was that?" Egon asked.

"Some crank"—Stantz sighed—"looking for goat hooves. Come up with anything?"

Spengler cradled a book in his hands. "This one is interesting. Berlin, 1939. A flower cart took off by itself and rolled approximately half a kilometer over level ground. Three hundred eyewitnesses."

Ray Stantz took a toxic puff of his pipe. "Hmmmm. You might want to check the *A.S.P.R.,* volume six, number three, 1968–1969, Renzacker and Buell, Duke University, mean averaging study on controlled psychokinetics."

Spengler nodded enthusiastically. He had missed working with Ray. "Oh, *yes.* That's a good one."

The front door suddenly flew open, sending the tiny bone chimes above it clanking. Peter Venkman strode in, wiggling his eyebrows at Ray. "Oh, hello, perhaps you could help me. I'm looking for an aerosol love potion I could spray on a certain *Penthouse* Pet that would make her unconditionally submit to an *unusual* personal request."

Stantz continued to brew his tea. "Oh, hiya, Pete."

Venkman walked up to the counter. "So, no goat hooves, huh?"

Stantz was stunned. "I *knew* that voice sounded familiar. What's up? How's it going?"

"Nowhere . . . fast," Venkman replied, staring at the piles of old books around him. "Why don't you lock up and buy me a sub?"

Ray was bad at being evasive, but he gave it his best shot. "Uh, I can't. I'm kind of working on something."

Spengler chose that moment to step out from behind the stacks of books on the paranormal.

Venkman extended his arms in a mock embrace. "Egon!"

"Hello, Venkman." Spengler frowned.

Venkman trotted over to Egon and put an arm around the man's shoulders. "How've you been? What are you up to? You never call, Egon. Shame on you."

"You don't have a phone," Spengler replied logically.

"Oh, yeah, right." Venkman nodded. "Well, I'm negotiating with AT&T right now. So how's teaching? I bet those science chicks really dig that big cranium of yours, huh? Ooooh."

"I think they're more interested in my epididymis," Spengler answered.

Venkman flinched. "I don't even want to know what that is."

Venkman strolled behind Ray's counter and, reaching into a mini-fridge, removed and popped open a beer. He began guzzling it.

Stantz was clearly nervous having Venkman in the store. "Oh, uh, your book came in, Venkman." He reached behind the counter and produced a large paperback. "*Magical Paths to Fortune and Power.*"

Venkman took the book and began rifling through the table of contents. "Hmm. Interesting material here. Money. More money. Even more money. See: Donald Trump."

He glanced at Stantz. "So what are you guys working on?"

Stantz swallowed hard, flashing a nervous look at

Egon Spengler. "Umm, just checking something out for an old friend."

Venkman leaned over the counter. "Who?"

Stantz began to sweat. "Who? It's . . . just someone we know."

Stantz slumped down on the stool as Venkman stood above him, a twisted smile on his face. "Oh, Ray. I am heartbroken."

"Y-you are?" Stantz gulped.

Venkman shook his head from side to side. "Truly. I have this horrible, awful, *terrible* feeling that you, one of my oldest and closest friends, are hiding something from me."

Egon rolled his eyes. "Oh, brother."

Venkman, still smiling, reached down and grabbed Ray by the ears. He pulled Ray up off his perch by his earlobes. "Who is it, Ray? Who? Who? Who?"

"Aaaah!" Ray yelled, his ears now extended enough to qualify him for a free pass to Disneyland. "Nobody! I mean, somebody! I mean, *I can't tell you*!?"

"Who, Ray?" Venkman cooed, his hands still firmly attached to Ray's ears.

"*Dana!*" Ray blurted. "*Dana Barrett!*"

Venkman let go of Ray's ears and smiled. Spengler stared at Stantz with disgust.

"Thank you, Ray." Venkman smiled. "You are one heck of a good friend . . . and I mean that from the heart."

7

Dana stood in the bedroom door and watched Maria, the young Hispanic woman who provided day-care service for her, feed little Oscar in the kitchen. Everything had seemed to go all right since Oscar's buggy decided to go rock and rolling across town, but still, Dana was worried.

When her front doorbell chimed, she instinctively knew that help was on the way.

"I'll get it, Maria," she said, rushing toward the door and flinging it open. Outside, in the hallway, were Ray and Egon.

"Ray," she said, hugging the tall Ghostbuster. "It's good to see you. Thanks for coming."

Stantz was slightly embarrassed. "No problem. Always glad to help . . . and hug."

"Hi, Egon," she said, shaking the bespectacled scientist's hand. She let them into her tastefully furnished apartment and was about to close the door when she heard a familiar voice.

"Hi, Dana."

Dana gulped, suddenly feeling as if she had a few hamsters doing treadmill tricks in her stomach.

Peter Venkman stepped into her doorway, wagging a "naughty, naughty" finger in the air. "I *knew* you'd come crawling back to me."

Dana found herself smiling, in spite of her shock. She was always both amazed and amused at how quickly Venkman's mouth formed words. She often wondered if his brain ever had the time to catch up. "Hello, Peter," she said with a sigh.

Venkman stepped inside the apartment. "You know, Dana. I'm very, very hurt that you didn't call me first. I'm still into all this stuff, you know. In fact, I'm considered an expert. Haven't you ever seen my TV show?"

"I have." Dana nodded coolly. "That's why I didn't call you first."

Venkman clutched his heart, as if mortally wounded by an arrow. He gazed at the ceiling. "I can see that you're still very bitter about us," he said.

Then he added with a shrug, "But in the interests of science I'm going to give it my best shot. Let's go to work, boys."

Stantz and Spengler rolled their eyes. It seemed just like old times . . . unfortunately. The two former Ghostbusters produced their small PKE measuring devices, hand-held creations that looked a tad like electric razors with wings. They carefully passed the monitors over and around little Oscar before checking out the rest of the apartment for any residual psychokinetic energy.

Venkman, leaving the others to handle the hardcore science, thrust his hands in his pockets and decided to give himself a tour of Dana's apartment.

He nodded as he checked out the furniture. Pretty nice. It sure beat the raunchy stuff he was using right now. He gazed meaningfully at Dana's plush couch. Up until last week he had been using a series of packing crates to sit on. It must be nice not to get splinters sitting on a couch.

"So," he said casually, "what happened to Mr. Right? I hear he ditched you and the kid and moved to Europe."

"He didn't 'ditch' me," Dana said, bristling. "We had some . . . problems. He got a good offer from a company in England and he took it."

Venkman held his smile. "He ditched you. You should've married me, you know."

"You never asked me," Dana shot back. "And every time I brought it up, you'd get drowsy and fall asleep."

Venkman seemed shocked. "Hey, men are *very* sensitive, you know. We need to feel loved and desired too."

"Well"—Dana smiled thinly—"when you started introducing me as 'the old ball and chain,' that's when I left."

Venkman saw the logic in this. "I may have a few personal problems," he admitted, "but one thing I am is a total professional."

He marched meaningfully across the room to Spengler. Egon had little Oscar sprawled on the couch and was in the middle of taking a complete set of body and head measurements of the lad, using a tape measure and calipers. Venkman was intrigued.

"What are you going to do, Egon? Knit him a snowsuit?"

Spengler ignored the remark and handed Venkman a small jar. "I'd like to have a stool specimen," he muttered.

"Yeah, you would," Venkman agreed. "Is that for personal or professional reasons?"

Spengler shot Venkman a look that equaled the phrase *zip it.* Venkman withered into silence. He gazed down at little Oscar. He had never seen a baby so close-up before. He tilted his head down at the boy. Was the kid smiling at him?

He picked up the baby in his hands. "Okay, kid. Up you go."

He held the giggling baby over his head and pressed his nose into the baby's belly, making the baby laugh even more.

"He's attacking!" Venkman cried. "Help! Please, somebody help me! Get him off! Quickly! He's gone completely berserk."

Ray and Egon sighed and smiled, continuing their readings of the house. Dana was mildly surprised at Venkman's latent daddy prowess.

"What do you think?" she asked him as Venkman continued to clown with the baby.

"There's no doubt about it," Venkman said, staring into the boy's cherubic face. "He's got his father's looks. The kid is ugly . . . extremely ugly. And smelly."

Venkman grinned at the baby and jiggled him. The baby whooped with glee. "You stink, baby. It's just horrible. You are the stinkiest baby I ever smelled."

He turned to Dana. "What's his name?"

"His name is Oscar."

Venkman flashed a sad smirk at Oscar. "You poor kid."

Dana finally lost her patience with Venkman's kidding. "Peter, this is serious. I need to know if you think there's anything unusual about him."

Venkman held Oscar directly in front of him. "Hmm. Unusual? I don't know. I haven't had a lot of experience with babies."

"Sample?" Spengler reminded him from across the room.

"Right." Venkman nodded.

Venkman laid the baby down on the couch and attempted to remove its little sleeper. He wasn't sure whether to pull it down over the child's feet or up over its head. Oh, well, he figured. He had a fifty-fifty chance of getting it right.

Dana snatched the jar away from him. "I'll do it," she snapped.

"I'll supervise." He smiled.

"You'll do no such thing," she said.

"Right." Venkman nodded, seeing Oscar's diaper. "I'll do no such thing."

Venkman strolled into Oscar's nursery, where Ray Stantz was carefully monitoring every piece of furniture and every toy for traces of psychokinetic energy. Venkman sidled up to Ray. Ray rubbed his groundhog hair, puzzled.

"Well, Holmes," Venkman asked. "What do you think?"

"It's an interesting one, Pete. If anything was going on, it's totally subdued now."

Egon Spengler entered the room, similarly confused.

Venkman recognized the look. Intense concentration. "What now, brainiac?"

"I think we should see if we can find anything abnormal on the street," he said.

Venkman nodded. "Finding something abnormal on a New York street shouldn't be too hard."

Moments later Dana Barrett was leading Stantz, Spengler, and Venkman down East Seventy-seventh Street, carefully retracing the route Oscar's baby buggy had taken after it developed a mind of its own. Stantz and Spengler worked in silence, monitoring the PKE valences from the pavement and the buildings.

Venkman ignored them, chatting up Dana as he

gazed up and down the street. "Brings back a lot of sweet memories, doesn't it?" he said, waxing nostalgic.

He pointed to several points of interest. "There's our old cash machine. And the dry cleaners we used to go to. And the old video store."

Venkman heaved a phony sob and wiped a nonexistent tear from his eye. "We really had some good times, didn't we?"

"We definitely had a moment or two," Dana said. She suddenly stopped at the intersection and pointed to the middle of the street. "That's where the buggy stopped."

Venkman stared at the street. "Okay. Let's take a look."

Venkman stepped out into moving traffic, ignoring the DON'T WALK sign and the cars whizzing around him. He held up his arms and began rerouting traffic like a cop would.

"Okay, buddy," he said sternly. "Slow it down. And you? Back it up. Aha! Caught you. Simon didn't say 'Back it up.' "

He motioned for Dana, Stantz, and Spengler to join him in the middle of the street. "Okay, kids. It's safe to cross now."

Stantz was the first to arrive. "Is this the spot?"

Dana extended a finger. "A little to the left."

Stantz moved his PKE monitor slightly.

"Right there!" Dana exclaimed. "That's where it stopped."

Stantz read the meter. "Nothing," he said, puzzled. "Not a trace."

Spengler lapsed into his *more* intense concentration mode. "Why don't we try the Giga meter?"

"What's that?" Venkman blinked.

Traffic was at a standstill for blocks now. Venkman ignored the honking cars and screaming drivers.

"Egon and I have been working on a gauge to measure psychomagnetheric energy in GEVs," Stantz explained. "Giga electron volts."

"That's a thousand million electron volts," Spengler clarified.

Venkman nodded sagely. "I knew that."

Spengler reached into his small carrying bag and removed the small machine he had demonstrated for Dana earlier in his lab. He passed the small device over the spot in the street where little Oscar's buggy had come to a sudden stop. Egon's eyes grew wide as the machine began to click wildly, and the GEV indicator shot into the red zone and stuck there.

Stantz gazed over Egon's shoulder, gaping. "I think we hit the honey pot, folks. There's something brewing under the street."

Dana gulped, glancing at Venkman. "Peter," she said, her voice trembling. "Do you think maybe I have some genetic problems or something that makes me vulnerable to these supernatural things?"

Venkman put a reassuring arm around her shoulders. "You mean like the time you got possessed and turned into a monster terror dog? Naaaah. Not a chance. Total coincidence."

He smiled at Stantz and Spengler. "Am I right?"

Stantz and Spengler looked first at each other, and then at Venkman. They were clearly not buying the coincidence theory.

"I said," Venkman repeated, " 'Am I right?' "

"Oh, yeah," Stantz nodded.

"Sure," Spengler agreed.

Venkman led Dana, Spengler, and Stantz back to the curb. He faced the frozen traffic behind him. "Gentlemen!" he called. "Start your engines."

Within seconds, traffic on East Seventy-seventh Street was as frantic as usual. The New York street once again looked perfectly normal . . . for now.

8

The late-afternoon sun shed an orange glow on the Manhattan Museum of Art as dusk began to fall. Cheerful security guards ushered the last guests out of the vast museum complex while other workers shut the museum's huge glass doors for the day.

In the back of the museum, in the restoration studio, wiry Janosz Poha didn't notice the time.

He continued to work on the gigantic painting of Vigo, one of the cruelest dictators in the history of the Western world. He was disturbed momentarily by Rudy, one of the museum's security guards. Rudy was a third-generation New Yorker, an Irishman whose father and grandfather had been cops. He'd always loved art, so he managed to combine his two callings by becoming an "art cop."

Rudy, making his early-evening rounds, looked up as Janosz worked carefully on restoring the ugly painting. Rudy didn't exactly know art, but he knew what gave him the willies. That painting gave him the willies.

"Oh, hello, Mr. Poha." Rudy smiled. "You working late today?"

Poha attempted a carefree grin. It looked as if he had just backed into a live wire. "Huh? Oh, yes, Rudy. I'm working on a very important painting."

Rudy looked at the canvas. Spook-house stuff, if you asked him. Still, Poha was supposed to be a pretty bright young guy. "Just be sure to sign out when you leave," he said, turning his back on the portrait of the mighty warrior.

Janosz went back to his restoration work. High above him, the eyes of Vigo of Carpathia slowly flickered to life. Vigo stared down at the tiny mortal working far below his eyes. An evil grin twisted across his lips.

Janosz, unaware that he was being watched, once more raised his brush to the canvas. He screamed in terror as a powerful bolt of blood-red, crackling energy hit the brush full blast. The bolt of power shot through the brush and wormed its way through Janosz's body, forcing the confused artist to his knees.

Groggy from the sudden charge, Janosz gazed up at the visage of Vigo.

He rubbed his eyes in disbelief.

The entire painting seemed to come alive.

Vigo slowly lowered his massive head and sneered at the cowering collection of flesh and blood trembling before him. "I am Vigo," he announced in a voice that resonated like thunder, "the Scourge of Carpathia, the Sorrow of Moldavia. I, Vigo, command you."

Janosz was mesmerized. "Command me, Lord," he whispered.

Vigo smiled at his newfound servant. "On a mountain of skulls in a castle of pain, I sat on a throne of blood. Twenty thousand corpses swung from my walls and parapets, and the rivers ran with tears."

Janosz nodded dumbly. Yes, that sounded like Vigo's hometown, all right.

"By the power of the Book of Gombots," Vigo thundered, "what *was* will *be,* what *is* will be *no more*! Past and future, now and ever, my time is near. Now is the season of *evil.* Find me a *child* that I may *live* again!"

Two jagged streams of crimson energy emerged from Vigo's baleful eyes and swirled down toward hapless Janosz. Janosz tried to scream but could not. He tried to move but could not. The bolts of energy smashed into Janosz's eyes, sending the cowering man sinking farther down onto the floor.

His consciousness swam.

He found himself getting to his feet.

He stared at the painting of Vigo. It was quiet now. Janosz clenched his teeth. He felt new confidence. New power. He had been given a command.

He knew what to do.

He knew how to make Vigo happy.

He knew how to make Vigo powerful.

And if he was a very good servant, perhaps he, too, would share in Vigo's glory.

Janosz marched out of the restoration studio and through the darkened corridors of the museum.

He strode toward the rear exit of the building, past the security-guard station, and out the door, leaving a bewildered Rudy sitting at his security desk, pen in hand.

"Hey! Mr. Poha!"

Rudy watched the wiry artist disappear into the night.

Rudy shook his head sadly. Eggheads. "I knew he'd forget to sign out." He sighed.

In the darkness of Manhattan, Janosz walked calmly, his eyes ablaze with Vigo's power.

They shone a bright, bloody red.

9

Venkman and Stantz emerged from an all-night coffee shop on East Seventy-seventh Street as a cold wind howled through the dark canyons of Manhattan. Carrying a small armful of pastries, sandwiches, and coffee, Venkman was the picture of enthusiasm . . . a concept that made Ray Stantz nervous. He had seen Venkman like this before. When Venkman was happy, trouble was on the way.

"I love this," Venkman said, gushing. "We're on to something really big, Ray. I can smell it. We're going to make some headlines with this one."

Ray Stantz frowned. "Hey, hey, hey, stresshound! Are you nuts?"

Venkman pondered the query but didn't reply.

"Have you forgotten we're under a judicial restraining order?" Stantz pointed out. "The judge couldn't have been clearer—no, I repeat, no ghostbusting. If anybody found out about this, we'd be in serious trouble. If we're going to do this for Dana, we've got to keep this whole thing low-key, low-profile, nice and quiet."

43

"What?" Venkman replied. "I can't hear you!"

Stantz winced. Venkman *couldn't* hear him, and the reason was standing three yards away. Egon Spengler, wearing a hard hat and work clothes, stood in the middle of the intersection pounding a hole in the street with a huge jackhammer. Safety cones and reflectors had been set up, and Egon had lit the whole area with powerful work lights.

Stantz handed Venkman his half-chewed Danish and walked into the work area, tapping Spengler on the back. Spengler nodded and handed Stantz the hard hat and the jackhammer. Ray took a deep breath and proceeded to rip the street to shreds.

Egon walked wearily over to Venkman, rubbing his sore right shoulder. Venkman smiled and handed him a cup of coffee. Egon wasn't overly impressed. "You were supposed to help me with this."

"You need the exercise," Venkman replied.

The two men put down their coffees and sandwiches and stood, picks and shovels at hand, ready to clear the rubble.

Venkman glanced over his shoulder.

A police cruiser was slowly making its way up the street toward the men's impromptu construction site. Venkman heaved a sigh. There was always a cop around when you didn't need one.

Stantz, in the middle of the road jackhammering away, didn't see or hear the police car approach.

The two cops brought the car to a halt directly behind Stantz and waited.

Stantz, noticing a new source of illumination behind him, stopped the jackhammer. He heard a car idling very close behind him. He turned and, flashing a smile known only to beauty queens and politicians, froze in his tracks.

"How ya doin'!" one of the cops yelled from inside the patrol car.

Stantz began to sweat. "Fine!" he said, his mind reeling. "It's cutting fine now."

The cop inside the car considered this and frowned. "Um," he offered, "*why* are you cutting?"

Stantz glanced over at Spengler and Venkman. Venkman offered a beats-me expression.

Ray began to lose it. "Why are we cutting? That's a great question, Officer."

He turned sweetly to Venkman. "Uh, *boss?*"

Venkman tossed on a Consolidated Edison hard hat and, his lips working overtime, executed a fine imitation of a typical New York Con Ed repairman.

"What's the trouble?" he groused, ambling over toward the squad car.

"What are you doing here?" the cop asked.

"What the hell's it look like we're doing?" Venkman spat.

The cop was dumbfounded.

"I tell you what the hell we're doing," Venkman continued. "We're bustin' our butts over here 'cause some *nitwit* downtown ain't got nothin' better to do than make idiots like us work late on a Friday night. Right, Rocky?"

He faced Egon Spengler. Spengler nervously raised a fist. "Yo!" he barked, stymied.

The cops in the car nodded, accepting the explanation.

"Okay, boys." The driver of the patrol car nodded. "Take it easy."

The patrol car puttered away. Ray Stantz heaved a mighty sigh of relief, trying to get his heart to stop pounding through his work clothes. Taking a deep breath, he hunkered over the jackhammer and began pounding into the street again.

Bzzzzark.

The jackhammer stammered to a stop.

"I've hit something, guys," Stantz called. "Something metal."

Spengler and Venkman used their picks and shovels to clear away generations of paving material. There, at the bottom of the hole, was an ornate iron manhole cover. Stantz stared at the ancient slab of circular metal. On its top was engraved a strange logo, along with the letters NYPRR.

Stantz squinted at the weird manhole cover. "NYPRR? What the heck does that mean? Help me lift this."

Venkman and Spengler picked up crowbars and removed the manhole cover from the bottom strata of street. Stantz produced a flashlight and peered down into the dankness.

"Wow!" he theorized. "It's an old air shaft! It goes on forever!"

Spengler pushed his head inside the hole, along with his Giga meter. The indicator on the meter nearly flew off the machine. "Very intense," he said thoughtfully. "We need a deeper reading. *Somebody* has to go down there."

Venkman smiled at Stantz. "I nominate Ray."

"I second," Egon blurted.

"All in favor?" Venkman injected before Ray could respond.

"Aye," both Venkman and Spengler chorused.

Venkman turned to Stantz and pumped his hand. "Congratulations, Ray. *You* are nominated. You're one lucky guy."

Stantz nodded sadly. "Thanks, boys."

Standing as forlornly as a child being snapped into a bulky snowsuit, Ray Stantz allowed himself to be strapped into a harness by Venkman and Spengler. A cable attached to a huge winch was secured to his back. Ray strapped to his belt a radio, the Giga meter, and a small extension hook with a scooping device.

He sighed and climbed into the manhole, his companions slowly cranking him down into the darkness.

"Is that dedication or what?" Venkman said to Spengler.

"Keep going," Ray called from the shaft. "More. More. Easy does it."

Inside the seemingly endless air shaft, Stantz rappeled off the metallic walls, descending slowly into a land of total darkness.

Stantz, unable to yell up to the surface, grabbed his radio. "I'm okay," he reassured Venkman and Spengler. "Lower . . . lower."

He flicked off the radio and gazed into the murkiness around him. "Gee," he concluded sagely, "this is really deep."

Suddenly he felt himself kicking against thin air. The long shaft had ended. Stantz found himself spinning wildly at the top of some titanic tunnel. Stantz felt like a yo-yo on its last big spin.

"Hold it!" he cried into the radio. "Hold it."

The cable stopped moving.

Ray pulled out the powerful flashlight from his utility belt and, flicking it on, aimed it at the vast tunnel below.

Ray suppressed a gasp. He was dangling near the top of a beautifully preserved chamber with rounded, polished tile walls adorned with intricate, colorfully enameled Art Nouveau mosaics. Ray felt as if he had just leapt backward in time. He trained the flashlight on a finely inlaid sign that identified the location. VAN HORNE STATION.

Ray whistled through his teeth, scanning the walls with his flashlight.

The place looked like a subway passenger's vision of heaven.

Smiling to himself, he raised his radio. "This is it, boys," he whispered reverently. "The end of the line. Van Horne Station. The old New York Pneumatic. It's still here."

Aboveground, Venkman shot a puzzled glance at Egon. "The New York Pneumatic Railway," Spengler explained. "It was an experimental subway system, composed of fan-forced air trains. It was built around 1870."

Ray's voice crackled over the radio. "This is about as deep as you can go under Manhattan without digging your own hole."

Spengler cradled the walkie-talkie in his hands. "What's the reading, Ray?"

Belowground, Stantz shone his flashlight onto the Giga meter. The meter was going crazy. He whistled into his radio. "Off the top of the scale, Egon. This place is really _hot._ Lower me to the floor, will ya?"

Stantz felt the cable quiver.

Soon he was being lowered closer to the old tunnel's floor. He slowly scanned the area with his flashlight, eventually spotlighting the floor.

Stantz's eyes grew wide in terror. "Hold it!" he yelled into the radio. "Stop! Whoa!"

In the beam of his flashlight, Stantz saw not a solid floor below him, but rather a river of bubbling, pulsating, glowing slime. A torrent of disgusting ooze.

The cable jerked to a halt.

Stantz found himself dangling above the torrent of psychokinetic mucus.

He lifted his feet as high into the air as he could, to avoid the splats of slime emitted by the constantly churning river.

Sweat began to form on his forehead. Gradually he became aware of the sounds of the city echoing around him: engines throbbing and pulsing in the bowels of the city; water rushing through pipes; steam hissing through air ducts; the muffled rumble of the ever-grinding subways; and the roar of traffic high above.

What Ray noticed most, however, were the echoes of people in conflict and pain. Voices of citizens shouting in anger, screaming in fear, groaning in agony. Ray sagged under the weight of the sad and eerie chorus.

Suddenly Ray's walkie-talkie barked to life. "What is it?" asked Spengler from above.

Ray grimaced into the ooze. "It's a seething, bubbling psychic cesspool," he blurted. "Interlocked tubes of plasm, crackling with negative GEVs. It's glowing and moving! It's . . . it's a river of slime!"

"Yccch," he heard Venkman comment from above.

Stantz gritted his teeth. He had a job to do down here. He unhooked a long, slender device from his utility belt and pulled a trigger on it. The device shot out a long, telescoping fishing pole with a plastic scoop on the end. Reaching down tentatively, Stantz scooped up a sample of the slime and carefully started reeling it in.

The ooze beneath his feet began to churn and turn.

Without warning, a grotesque arm of slime reached up toward Ray, extending its glistening, skeletal fingers in the direction of Stantz's dangling feet. Ray screeched and jerked his legs up high into the air as other hands of ooze bubbled upward, reaching for him, clawing at him. Ray found himself squirming at the end of the cable in a near fetal position. He felt like a piñata from another dimension.

"Haul me up, Venkman!" he bellowed into the radio. "Now!"

On Seventy-seventh Street, Venkman and Spengler ran to the winch and started to crank the cable upward. Just as they began their rescue attempt, a Con Ed supervisor's car pulled up. Behind it was the same police car that had patrolled the area earlier. Venkman and Spengler exchanged nervous glances.

"What now?" Spengler asked.

"Act like nothing is wrong," Venkman advised.

The burly Con Ed supervisor rumbled up to the two men, followed by the pair of cops.

"Okay," the man demanded, "what's going on here?"

Venkman and Spengler stopped pulling up the cable. Venkman quickly doffed his Con Ed hard hat and put on a phone-company helmet. He stared angrily at the Con Ed man.

"What, I got time for this?" he blustered. "We got three thousand phones out in the Village and about eight million miles of cable to check."

The Con Ed man smiled thinly. "The phone lines are over there," he said, pointing toward the curb.

Venkman turned to Spengler and, forming a fist, hit him over the head. "I told ya!"

Stantz's voice suddenly emerged from the walkie-talkie. "Help! Help! Pull me up! It's alive! It's eating my boots."

Venkman offered the cops a quick grin and switched off the radio. "You ain't with Con Ed," the first cop concluded, "*or* the phone company. We checked. Tell me another one."

Venkman scanned his brain for a comeback. He faced the cop. "How does a gas leak sound?"

Down below the street, caught halfway up the air shaft, Stantz gazed at the scene unfolding beneath his feet. The slime was now bubbling up the air shaft after him. The ooze seemed angry. Determined. Hungry.

Stantz panicked. Nobody was receiving him over the radio. He gazed upward at the tiny manhole opening, far, far above him. "Get me out of here!" he screamed.

No response.

Desperation and fear getting the best of him, Stantz began kicking wildly at the air shaft. The old metal began to creak and groan under the assault by Stantz's boots.

A section of an old conduit came loose and began to topple over.

Stantz watched its journey, befuddled. "Uh-oh," he whispered.

The conduit fell on a heavy electrical transmission line. It ripped through the cable neatly. A shower of sparks lit up the air vent.

"Definitely uh-oh," Stantz theorized as the sparks seemed to illuminate every underground passageway extending outward from the air shaft.

Venkman was in the midst of attempting to sell the police another story when there was a sudden buzzing sound from deep within the open manhole.

Venkman and Spengler exchanged worried looks as Stantz's shouts emerged from deep beneath the city streets.

"Whooaaaah!" Stantz exclaimed.

"What the—" the Con Ed man had time to offer before, one by one, all the lights on the street flickered and then went out.

Then all the lights in the neighborhood followed suit.

The cops, the Con Ed man, and the two Ghostbusters watched in awe as, neighborhood by neighborhood, all of New York was plunged into total darkness.

From deep within the earth came a feeble voice, the voice of Ray Stantz.

"Sorry," he said.

10

As the lights flickered out all over New York City, Dana Barrett suddenly found herself engulfed in darkness. Always prepared, she felt her way around the living room, lighting various candles she had left out for just such an occasion.

Locating a small transistor radio, she turned it on and tried to find a special news report.

She had tuned in too quickly.

Most of the radio stations in New York were still scrambling to turn on their emergency generators.

Dana suddenly felt the overwhelming compulsion to check on little Oscar.

Grabbing a candle, she began to tiptoe toward the nursery when she was interrupted by a pounding on her front door.

Candle still in hand, she walked cautiously to the door and, leaving the guard chain on, opened it a crack. Outside, the hallway, eerily lit by a dim red emergency spotlight at the far end of the corridor, offered a visitor.

A hyper, wiry man.

"Janosz?" she asked.

Janosz smiled at her. "Hello, Dana. I happened to be in the neighborhood and I thought I'd stop by to see if everything was all right with you. You know, with the blackout and everything? Are you okay? Is . . . *the baby* . . . all right?"

Dana felt a chill insinuate itself down her spine. She put up a nonchalant front. "We're fine, Janosz."

The minion of Vigo tried to stick his head farther inside the chained door, hoping to scan the apartment. "Do you need anything?" he said, still grinning. "Would you like me to come in?"

"No," Dana replied a little too quickly. "Everything is fine. Honestly. Thanks, anyway."

Janosz took the refusal in stride. "Okay. Just thought I'd check. Good night, Dana. Sleep well. don't let the bedbugs *bite* you."

"Good night, Janosz," Dana breathed, easing the door closed. She stood there, panting. There was something about Janosz. He had always been weird, but now he struck her as being *weirder*. She quickly double-locked the door.

She stood in the middle of her candlelit apartment.

Very alone.

Very afraid.

Outside Dana's door, Janosz smiled evilly at the closed portal.

Closed doors didn't bother him.

Locks meant nothing to him.

He had a job to do, and in time he would do it.

Janosz turned and gazed down the darkened corridor. Blackouts. Hah! He reached deep down into himself and touched the power within. Slowly his eyes began to flicker . . . then to shine brightly.

Small beams of crimson-red energy lit up the hall enough for Janosz to walk down it without stumbling.

It was good to have a friend.

And Vigo was his best friend, *ever.*

11

By morning, New York City had its power restored, and Spengler, Stantz, and Venkman had their hands full.

They sat in a courtroom, sharing the defense table with Louis Tully, C.P.A., perpetual target of a bad haircut, former demonic possession victim, and now lawyer extraordinaire, thanks to a quick course in the Famous Lawyer's School and Dry Cleaning Emporium.

Louis Tully pushed his glasses higher on his nose, which in turn made his nose run. He pulled out a hankie from his badly cut suit, which caused the plastic pen holder to tumble out of his pocket onto the floor.

"S'cuse me." he muttered to the three Ghostbusters as he stooped to pick up his pens, nearly knocking over a pitcher of water on the defense table.

Across from him, the prosecuting attorney, an attractive young woman who seemed to want to see Spengler, Stantz, and Venkman hanged, glared at Louis.

Louis quickly straightened himself and began poring through an avalanche of law books he had gathered for the occasion.

"All rise," the bailiff said.

Everyone in the courtroom stood as Judge Roy Beane strode into the room. A compact, balding man with the deep eyes of a ferret and a small, neatly trimmed mustache, the judge gaveled the court into session.

The three Ghostbusters slid into their seats as the judge began. "I want to make one thing very clear before we go any further," he said severely.

"The law does not recognize the existence of ghosts, and I don't believe in them, either. So . . . I don't want to hear a lot of malarkey about goblins and spooks and demons. We're going to stick to the facts in this case and save the ghost stories for the kiddies. Understood?"

"Understood, Your Honor," the prosecutor said with a grin.

"Uh-huh," Louis muttered.

Stantz leaned over toward Spengler. "Seems like a pretty open-minded guy, huh?"

Egon nodded, the hair on the back of his neck bristling. "His nickname is the Hammer."

Venkman spotted Dana in the visitors' gallery and slowly backed toward her, leaving Spengler and Stantz trapped with Louis. Louis nervously glanced up at Spengler. His voice was in high-whine mode. "I think you're making a big mistake here, fellas. I do mostly tax law, and some probate stuff occasionally. I got my law degree at night school."

"That's all right," Egon reassured him. "We got arrested at night."

Venkman and Dana exchanged looks. "I wish I

could stay," Dana whispered. "I feel personally responsible for you being here."

"You *are* personally responsible. If I can get conjugal rights, will you visit me at Sing Sing?"

"Please don't say that!" Dana blurted. "You won't go to prison."

Venkman puffed out his chest. "Don't worry about me. I'm like a cat."

"You mean you cough up hairballs all over the rug?"

Venkman shot her a look. "I'm El Gato. I always land on my feet."

"Good luck," Dana said, giving Venkman a quick, unexpected kiss before dashing out of the courtroom.

"Thanks," Venkman said, savoring the kiss for a long moment. He walked back to the defense table. Across the aisle, the mayor's top aide, Jack Hardemeyer, was goading the pretty prosecutor on for the kill.

Venkman strained his ears to listen.

"How are you doing, hon?" Hardemeyer asked. "Just put these guys away fast and make sure they go away for a long, long time."

Venkman wasn't pleased.

"It shouldn't be hard with this list of charges," the prosecutor replied.

Venkman sighed. He should have finished that Danish last night. It might be a long time before he experienced another one.

"Good." Hardemeyer smiled. "Very good. The mayor and future governor won't forget this."

Venkman scurried to his seat at the defense table. Hardemeyer made a major production of removing his well-groomed presence from the D.A.'s team and walking slowly past the defense table on his way out of the courtroom.

He looked down at Spengler, Stantz, and Venkman.

"Nice going, Venkman," he cooed. "Violating a judicial restraining order, willful destruction of public property, fraud, malicious mischief . . . smooth move. See you in a couple of years—at your first parole hearing."

Hardemeyer turned and marched out of the room. Louis watched the retreating figure, his face turning the color of damp chalk. "Gee, the whole city is against us. I think I'm going to be sick."

Spengler offered Louis a wastebasket as the prosecutor called her first witness.

The Con Ed supervisor took the stand.

Venkman sat at the table and began to doodle. He knew what was coming. He'd been railroaded before.

Venkman battled to keep from dozing off as the supervisor rattled off a list of crimes that he, Stantz, and Spengler had inflicted on the poor streets of New York.

He snapped to when he noticed a court employee carry some very familiar equipment into the room and place it on a nearby table.

The prosecutor was still hammering away at the Con Ed man. "Mr. Fianella," she said, "please look at Exhibits A through F on the table over there. Do you recognize that equipment?"

Spengler, Stantz, and Venkman exchanged uh-oh glances as the Con Ed man surveyed the table. There, spread out on its top, were the basic tools of the Ghostbusting trade. Three proton packs and particle throwers. A few unsprung ghost traps. The Giga and PKE meters.

The Con Ed man nodded vigorously. "That's the stuff the cops found in their rented van."

"Do you know what this equipment is for?" the prosecutor asked.

"I don't know." The burly man shrugged. "Catching ghosts, I guess."

The prosecutor whirled toward the judge. "May I remind the court that the defendants are under a judicial restraining order that *specifically* forbids them from performing services as paranormal investigators and eliminators?"

The judge with the ice-blue ferretlike eyes nodded. "Duly noted."

"Now," the prosecutor continued, "can you identify the substance in the jar on the table marked Exhibit F?"

She walked over to the exhibit table and picked up a large specimen jar. In it was housed the slime sample Stantz had removed from the swirling, churning tunnel floor.

The Con Ed man screwed up his face in confusion. "Lady," he said, "I been working underground for Con Ed for twenty-seven years and I never saw anything like that in my life. We checked out that tunnel real early this morning and we didn't find nothing. If it was down there, *they* must have put it down there."

Venkman and Spengler shot a suspicious look at Stantz. Ray withered under their gaze. "Hey," he said defensively, "I didn't imagine it. There must have been ten thousand gallons of it down there."

Egon Spengler stroked his square jaw. "It may be ebbing and flowing from some tidal source," he concluded.

Louis leaned toward the two men, nearly knocking over his books. "Should I say that?"

Spengler patted Louis's hand. "I doubt that they'd believe us."

Louis uttered a plaintive moan and slithered farther down in his chair. Why couldn't he have taken the dry-cleaning course instead of law? By now, he would have known what one-hour Martinizing really meant.

The Con Ed man was dismissed, and within minutes

Peter Venkman found himself on the stand, facing his own lawyer, the rattled, diminutive Louis. Louis had been babbling for about a minute, Venkman encouraging him with a helpful nod, a wink, or a hearty "Hear, hear." That gave Venkman the chance to think of what he would do when he was finally paroled. Not much, he concluded.

"S-so," Louis said, stammering. "Like you were just trying to help out your old friend because she was scared and you didn't really mean to do anything bad, and you really love the city and won't ever do anything like this again, right?"

Before a smiling, modest Venkman could reply, the prosecutor was on her feet. "Objection, Your Honor! He's leading the witness."

The judge glared at Venkman. "The witness is leading *him*. Sustained."

Louis blinked. "Ummm, okay. Let me rephrase that question."

Venkman smiled sweetly at Louis as the little man chirped, "Mr. Venkman, didn't you once coach a basketball team for underprivileged children?"

"Yes, I did," Venkman said proudly. "We were city champs."

"Objection!" the prosecutor spat. "Irrelevant and immaterial."

The judge sighed. "Sustained." He focused on Louis. "Mr. Tully, do you have anything to ask this witness that actually may have some *bearing* on this case?"

Louis turned to Venkman. "Do I?" he asked.

Venkman flashed Louis a reassuring smirk. "No, I think you've helped them enough already."

Louis shrugged at the judge. "No, I guess not. Your witness, Mrs. Prosecutress."

The prosecutor slowly rose out of her seat and

approached the witness stand. She was practically salivating over the prospect of destroying Venkman's credibility. Venkman was prepared. He had seen this kind of woman before. Actually he'd dated many of them in college.

"So," the prosecutor began. *"Doctor* Venkman, would you please explain to the court why it is that you and your codefendants took it upon yourselves to dig a big hole in the middle of the street?"

Venkman considered this. "Seventy-seventh and First Avenue has so many holes already, we didn't think anyone would notice."

The citizens gathered in the visitor's gallery laughed. The judge raised his gavel and hammered for order. He glowered at Venkman. "Keep that up, mister, and I'll find you in contempt!"

Venkman offered a shy grin. "Sorry, Your Honor, but when somebody sets me up like that, I just can't resist."

"I'll ask you again, Dr. Venkman," the prosecutor said, going in for the kill. "Why were you digging the hole? And please remember that you're under oath."

Venkman tried (unsuccessfully) to emulate Egon's very concerned mode. "I had my fingers crossed when they swore me in, but I'm going to tell you the truth. There are things in this world that go way beyond human understanding, things that can't be explained and that most people don't want to know about, anyway. That's where *we* come in."

Venkman nodded toward Spengler and Stantz.

"So what are you saying," the prosecutor asked, grinning like a barracuda. "That the world of the supernatural is your special province?"

"No," Venkman explained. "I guess I'm just saying that weird shit happens and *somebody* has got to deal with it."

The gallery began to cheer. Venkman took a bow. The judge gaveled for order.

Two hours later a frowning Venkman sat at the defense table. Stantz and Spengler had been similarly browbeaten on the witness stand, although, in Venkman's humble opinion, they didn't please the crowd *nearly* as much as he had.

The trial was now nearing its end. The judge nodded toward a trembling Louis to make his final summation.

"Does the counsel for the defense wish to make any final arguments?" he growled.

Louis slowly got to his feet, his knees knocking so hard that they sounded like Morse code. "Your Honor?" Louis squeaked, "may I approach the bench?"

"Yes, yes," the judge said impatiently.

Louis waddled over to the bench and gazed upward.

"What is it?" the judge demanded.

Louis gulped. "Can I have some of your water?"

"Get on with it, Counselor!"

Louis backed away from the bench and wasn't quite sure who to speak to. "Your Honor, ladies and gentlemen of the jury . . ."

"There's no jury here." The judge sighed.

". . . of the audience," Louis corrected himself, staring at the gallery. "I don't think it's fair to call my clients frauds. Okay. The blackout was a big problem for everybody. I was stuck in an elevator for about three hours and I had to go to the bathroom the whole time, but I don't blame them, because once I turned into a big dog and they helped me. Thank you."

Louis rushed back to the defense table and scrambled into his seat. Stantz and Spengler, dazed, stared at their knees in disbelief. Venkman leaned over the table and patted Louis on the back. "Way to go. Concise and to the point."

Obviously the judge was still in shock. He gazed at Louis. "That's *it*? That's *all* you have to say?"

Louis was confused. "Did I forget something?"

Louis began to plow through the hastily taken notes he had scrawled during the trial. The judge bared his teeth at the diminutive man. "That was unquestionably the worst presentation of a case I've ever heard in a court of law! I ought to cite you for contempt and have you disbarred. And as for your clients, Peter Venkman, Raymond Stantz, and Egon Spengler, on the charges of conspiracy, fraud, and the willful destruction of public property, I find you guilty on all counts. I order you to pay fines in the amount of $25,000 *each,* and I sentence you to eighteen months in the city correctional facility at Riker's Island!"

Stantz lifted his eyes. He caught a glimpse of the specimen jar, still perched on the exhibit table. The goop inside the jar began to glow and churn. He leaned toward Spengler. "Uh-oh. She's twitchin'."

The judge grew angrier and angrier with each word. The slime grew more and more animated as the judge's voice rose. "And on a more personal note," the judge intoned, "let me go on record as saying that there is no place in decent society for fakes, charlatans, and tricksters like you who prey on the gullibility of innocent people. You're beneath the contempt of this court!

"And believe me, if my hands were not tied by the unalterable fetters of the law, a law that has become, in my view, far too permissive and inadequate in its standards of punishment . . ."

The entire jar of slime seemed to change its shape, growing into something resembling an oval.

". . . I would invoke the tradition of our illustrious

forebears, reach back to a sterner, purer justice, and have you *all* burned at the stake!"

He slammed his gavel down on the bench. The gallery erupted into a chorus of boos and jeers. The judge was about to slam down his gavel again when he felt the floor beneath his massive desk begin to tremble.

The gallery lapsed into silence.

A low, rumbling noise grew in volume, echoing through the room.

The prosecutor glanced at the exhibit table. "What the . . ."

The slime began to pulse and swell in earnest, gradually forcing up the lid of the jar.

Stantz gaped at the jar.

The slime was moving quickly now, expanding at an incredible rate.

"Under the table, boys!" he yelled.

The three Ghostbusters dove under the table, yanking Louis under after them.

The rumbling increased to a deafening roar.

And that roar evolved into the psychic equivalent of a volcanic eruption of pure paranormal power.

"Wow," Stantz said, wide-eyed, as a hurricane-force wind from another dimension slammed into his face. "Isn't this *something*?"

12

A fierce, ethereal whirlwind whipped above the heads of Louis, Spengler, Stantz, and Venkman as the slime jar began to spout glowing, sparkling wads of goop up into the air.

A sizzling, undulating cloud of gooey vapor formed near the courthouse ceiling.

Aghast, the judge sat behind his desk, as two figures—one rotund, the other, emaciated—began to materialize high above. The judge recognized them immediately.

"Oh, my God," he whispered. "The Scoleri brothers!"

The ghostly Scoleri brothers, their fingers crackling electrical sparks, their hair sparking as well, glared down at the timid judge and emitted a loud eerie laugh. The two floating apparitions positioned themselves high above either side of the judge's massive desk and then, without warning, shrieked down into the desk, sending the large wooden frame sailing across the room in pieces.

The judge found himself sitting behind the smoldering ruins of his desk. The Scoleri brothers had dematerialized for the time being.

As the prosecutor stood stunned at her table, the spectators in court scrambled from their seats and ran for the back exit of the courtroom.

The judge, getting down on all fours, crawled toward the defense table and quickly rolled underneath it. Sweating and shaking, he faced Spengler, Stantz, and Veckman. "You've got to do something!" he cried.

"Who are they?" Venkman asked.

"They're the Scoleri brothers. I tried them for murder. They were electrocuted up at Ossining in '48. Now . . . they want to *kill* me!"

"Maybe they just want to appeal." Venkman shrugged.

"I don't think so." Louis moaned, watching the table slowly rise into the air above them.

From out of nowhere the Scoleri brothers materialized and, hair and fingertips crackling, the long dead criminals lifted the defense table high into the air!

"This way," Spengler yelled, pointing to the rail of the jury box. The three Ghostbusters, the judge, and Louis darted across the room and dove behind the heavy oak wall of the jury box.

The Scoleri brothers roared and sent the defense table smashing into the wall above their heads.

"These boys aren't playing around," Venkman noted.

The Scoleri brothers, still hovering near the ceiling, noticed the prosecutor for the first time. Exchanging ghostly glances, they began to hover closer to her. The woman let out a bloodcurdling scream. The Scoleris emitted a howling laugh and promptly disappeared.

The prosecutor exhaled and slowly began to back

toward the courtroom's exit doors, twisting and turning nervously, scanning the air above her for any sign of the angry apparitions.

She reached the door intact and, breathing a sigh of relief, reached for the door's handle.

She heard a crackling sound.

She smelled the aroma of ozone.

The woman's hair nearly straightened as suddenly the ghost of the skinny Scoleri brother sparked to life before her. The ghost emitted an unworldly screech as it blocked the door with its transparent body.

The prosecutor turned and ran toward the front of the courtroom, the skinny apparition following her. Before she could reach the jury box, she heard a strange rumbling noise. Pop! Blocking her path was the plumper ghost brother.

The big ghost glided forward.

The prosecutor froze in her tracks.

Hidden behind the jury box's railing, the judge pleaded with Stantz, Spengler, and Venkman. "You've got to stop them, please!"

Wide-eyed, Stantz blinked innocently at the judge. "I'm sorry, we can't. You issued a judicial restraining order that prohibits us from ghostbusting. Violating such an order could expose us to serious criminal penalties."

The judge blinked at honest, heartfelt Ray. A woman's scream cut through the air.

The judge slowly peeked over the jury-box railing. All color drained from his face. The titanic ghost of the obese Scoleri thug was calmly dragging the screeching prosecutor by her feet toward the rear of the courtroom, laughing and drooling devilishly.

The upside-down woman squirmed in the grip of

the spirit, trying desperately to keep her dress from sliding up over her head.

The exit doors to the courtroom mysteriously burst open. The fat ghost carried the screaming prosecutor out of the room, and as the doors swung closed, it vanished into thin air.

Behind the jury-box railing, the judge slowly sank into a sitting pose. He was defeated. "All right. All right. I'm rescinding the order. Case dismissed."

He noticed that he was still holding his gavel in his right hand. He pounded the floor judicially.

"Satisfied?"

"I guess so," Louis offered.

"Now," the judge said, fuming. *"Do something!"*

With that the three Ghostbusters leapt over the rail of the jury box and dashed across the room to the exhibit table. Their proton packs were lying there, tossed aside as useless evidence.

The three Ghostbusters strapped on their packs hastily, glancing above their heads for any signs of the Scoleri brothers.

Venkman felt like the Hunchback of Notre Dame as he affixed the pack to his back. "Geez, I forgot how heavy these things are."

Stantz cradled his particle thrower in his hand. "Okay"—he grinned at his long-lost high-tech friends—"let's heat 'em up."

The three Ghostbusters flipped on their proton-pack power switches in unison, then raised their particle throwers toward the ceiling.

"All right, throwers," Stantz barked, authority surging through his body. "Set for full neutronas on stream."

Stantz, Spengler, and Venkman switched on their throwers and raised them upward.

The throwers remained on standby. There was no sign of anything paranormal in the room.

All seemed quiet.

All seemed *normal.*

Suddenly, from the back of the courtroom came a ruckus. Chairs began to fly up into the air and then drop harmlessly to the floor. It seemed as if something were burrowing deep down underneath them, toward the front of the courtroom. Toward the Ghostbusters.

Stantz, Spengler, and Venkman stared at the courtroom before them.

There was nothing to be seen.

Stantz smiled thinly. Ghosts were goofy, perhaps, but pretty crafty. He stared at the empty ceiling above him.

"On my signal, gentlemen." He grinned.

He *felt* the Scoleri brothers nearby.

He was right.

A bolt of electrical energy shot across the ceiling above them and from out of the yellow mist appeared the gaunt and obese floating forms of the executed killers.

"Open 'em up!" Stantz yelled. *"Now!"*

The three Ghostbusters shut their eyes as their wands emitted squiggling, undulating, powerful streams of energy.

Not having used the weapons in four years, Spengler, Stantz, and Venkman fired wildly, allowing the harpy-like Scoleri ghosts to dodge the fluttering beams easily.

The ghosts emitted a ghastly cackle and then promptly dematerialized.

The Ghostbusters were too shaken to notice. They continued to fill the air with orange-hot rays. Venkman took out an overhead lamp. Spengler blew up the courtroom railing. Stantz managed to obliterate half of one of the courtroom's towering pillars.

The three Ghostbusters opened their eyes as one. "That ought to do it," Venkman said with a smirk. "Spengs, take the door. Ray, let's try to work them down and into a corner."

Working as a team, they fanned the area.

Spengler carefully backed up toward the exit doors.

Venkman cautiously circled the exhibit table, his weapon trained toward the ceiling.

Stantz walked to and fro before the jury box. The judge and Louis stayed well down behind the protective gate.

A howl shook the air.

The emaciated Scoleri ghost materialized from behind Stantz and lunged downward.

"Get down, Ray!" Venkman shouted as the ghost swooped down on his buddy.

Stantz leapt onto the ground and rolled out of the line of fire as Venkman let go with an undulating stream of rays that effectively trapped the screaming apparition within its force field.

"That's it, Venky!" Spengler yelled from the rear of the room. "Watch your streams. Hold him there."

Spengler moved toward the exhibit table, where two rectangular ghost trappers were set up, connected to five-foot-long cables attached to foot releases.

Spengler carefully moved the traps to the center of the courtroom.

"Easy, Venky," he cautioned.

"I got him." Venkman nodded nervously.

"Just keep the beam on him and ease him over there. Pull him down this way. That's it. That's it."

A shriek cut through the air. Spengler spun around and saw the ghost of the fat Scoleri bearing down upon him, fast. He couldn't reach his weapon in time to save himself.

Stantz leapt to his feet and opened fire. The fat ghost chortled with glee as he easily dodged the blast.

He headed down for Spengler once again.

Stantz gritted his teeth and let go with a second stream. This time the spiraling rays smashed into the fat ghost, effectively trapping him in a pulsating, levitating cage.

Spengler made sure there were *two* rectangular traps placed on the floor in front of what had once been the judge's bench.

He pulled the foot springs back some five feet.

Stantz and Venkman held the screaming ghosts trapped in their steady stream of rays.

"Okay," Spengler said, coaching them. "You're doing fine. Watch your streams. Easy, now. Venky, bring him left. Stantz, pull them down."

The two Ghostbusters nodded and slowly maneuvered their captive, screeching spirits down toward the rectangular traps.

Spengler watched their progress, sweating. "Okay. Trapping . . . trapping . . . *now!*"

Spengler stomped down hard on two foot-control pedals at the end of the pair of cables. The rectangular traps' top doors opened and a bright light streamed up from within.

Stantz and Venkman guided the two ghosts into the white-hot light.

"Cease fire!" Spengler yelped. "Now!"

An exhausted Stantz and Venkman lowered their weapons.

The two traps surged into full-tilt power, emitting an inverted triangle of ethereal light up toward the floating spirits. Gradually the ghosts dissipated, and then suddenly zipped into the two traps.

The traps snapped shut and an LED light on the outside of each trap flashed brilliantly.

Venkman staggered up to his trap. He smiled at Spengler. *"Ocupado."*

The three Ghostbusters faced each other, exhausted. They exchanged smiles. They hadn't felt this good in years.

The judge slowly stuck his head up from behind the jury box. Louis peeked up as well. The judge looked around in total shock.

Louis and the exhausted Ghostbusters walked to the back of the courtroom and flung open the door.

Outside, dozens of reporters and spectators waited to greet them with a rousing cheer.

Spengler glanced to his left. The prosecutor was hiding beneath a plastic chair, shivering her well-educated butt off. "Brilliant summation." He smiled.

Flashbulbs went off in the three men's faces.

Reporters surged forward.

Venkman faced his two comrades and uttered, loud enough for everyone to hear, "Case closed, boys. We're back in business."

The halls of the courthouse echoed with the cheers and applause of a devoted crowd.

II

"*True heroes are those who die for causes they cannot quite take seriously.*"

—MURRAY KEMPTON

•

"*This is going to cost you, you know. Our fees are ridiculously high.*"

—DR. PETER VENKMAN

13

The refurbished firehouse that once housed the original Ghostbusters business was under siege by a small army of workmen. The old "No Ghosts" logo, now dilapidated by years of disuse, came crashing to the ground with a resounding thud.

The workmen fought back sneezes as a cloud of dust wafted into the air.

A group of men struggled with a pulley as a new logo was hoisted into place over the main entrance of the building. It looked exactly like the old logo, but now the trapped ghost in the red circle held up two fingers.

Venkman strolled up to the firehouse and gazed at the Ghostbusters' shiny new symbol. Nice, he thought. Very, very nice.

Inside the firehouse's reception area, Janine Melnitz, a veteran New Yorker and the Ghostbusters' first (and only) receptionist/aide, hastily set up her desk. She spread out family photos. A Garfield doll. Bound editions of *Cosmopolitan*. She hardly noticed Louis as he waddled out with a handful of forms. Louis certainly noticed Janine. Why was it he had never seen how pretty she was? Oh, yeah, now he remembered. The last time he had been in the firehouse, he had been possessed by a demon.

Louis tiptoed up to Janine's desk, clearing his throat. He sounded like Shirley Temple with a hairball. "Uh, Janine? I'm filling out W-2 forms for the payroll and I need your Social Security number."

Janine carefully positioned her Garfield doll. "It's 129-45-8986."

Louis produced a small pad from his shirt pocket and jotted down the number. "Oh," he said, wheezing. "That's a good one. Mine is 322-36-7366."

Janine gazed up at Louis. You know, she thought, Louis was kind of cute in a *Wild Kingdom* sort of way. "Wow!" she exclaimed. "Three threes and three sixes."

"Uh-huh," Louis acknowledged.

"That's very strong in numerology," she continued, running a hand through her mousy brown hair. "It means you're a person with a great appetite for life and a *deeply passionate* nature."

Louis blinked, embarrassed. He almost fogged his glasses. "You can tell all that from my Social Security number?"

The sparrowlike Janine leaned forward and smiled. "Oh, yes. Numbers are very revealing. If I knew your phone number, I could tell you a lot more."

Louis swallowed hard. "My phone number?"

Venkman chose that moment to march into the room. Both Louis and Janine snapped to immediately.

"Louis, how are we doing on that bank loan?" Venkman asked.

Louis cleared his throat. "Oh, I called the bank this morning . . . but they hung up on me."

"Try another bank." Venkman shrugged. "Do I have to do *everything* around here?"

Venkman looked up as Stantz, Spengler, and Winston walked sheepishly downstairs wearing the Ghostbusters' uniforms Venkman had commissioned for their new incarnation. The uniforms were designed in a weirded-out, military style in Day-Glo colors, dripping with medals, and topped by ridiculous berets. Venkman took note of the trio's embarrassed faces and tried to bluff his way through it.

"Incredible!" he oozed. "*This* is a *very* good look!"

Winston heaved a heavy sigh. "We look like the Bronxville High School Marching Band."

Venkman sidled up to the trio. "Will you just *trust* me on this? It's all part of the new plan—higher visibility, lower overhead, deeper market penetration, *bigger profits.* Just wait until we open the boutique."

Stantz blinked. "What boutique?"

Venkman took him by the arm and pointed to the sky outside the firehouse. "The Ghostbusters Gift Boutique," he said enthusiastically. "It's a natural. I've been working on it all day."

He whipped a small piece of paper from his pants pocket and began reading. "You'll *love* it. Ghostbuster T-shirts, sweatshirts, caps, visors, beach towels, mugs, calendars, stationery, balloons, stickers, Frisbees, paperweights, souvenirs, tote bags, party supplies, motor oil, toys, video games."

Spengler frowned. "Our primary concern should be the continued integrity of the biosphere. It's a responsibility shared by all conscious beings."

Venkman stared at Spengler. "Isn't that what I just said?"

Stantz turned to Venkman. "Look, Venkman, we don't have time for this. We've got customers waiting—

paying customers. You can wear pink diapers and go-go boots if you want. *We're* sticking with the *old* coveralls."

The three Ghostbusters marched back up the stairs. Venkman trotted up behind them.

"Coveralls," he shouted. "Great! Very imaginative, Ray. They make us look like we should be walking around the airport sprinkling sawdust on puke!"

Stantz shouted down from above. "We're wearing them. And that's final!"

Venkman took this in and shouted up, with a smile, "Okay, we'll wear coveralls—but think *boutique*!"

14

The TV screen flickered to life displaying a very awkward married couple, played by Louis Tully and Janine, in bed, reading.

Suddenly a "ghost," actually a puppet that seemed to have been created in an out-therapy class in a laughing academy, bounced above the bed on a badly concealed wire.

Janine looked up and emitted a terribly acted scream.

"What is it, honey?" Louis blinked.

Janine crossed her arms and watched the puppet bounce off the plasterboard walls. "It's that darn ghost again," she said stiffly. "I don't know what to do anymore. He just won't leave us alone. I guess we'll just have to move."

Louis offered a wise smile, which resembled the one worn by Alfred E. Newman. "Don't worry, honey. *We're* not moving. *He* is."

Louis reached for the prop telephone.

"Who are you going to call?" Janine asked.

Louis winked at the screen. *"Ghostbusters."*

As Louis dialed, Spengler, Stantz, and Venkman marched into their room, clad in their old Ghostbusters jumpsuits. They walked as stiffly as wooden soldiers and weren't any better actors than Louis and Janine.

The threesome faced the screen.

"I'm Ray."

"I'm Peter."

"I'm Egon."

Stantz took a deep breath. "And we're the . . ."

"Ghostbusters!" the three men announced in unison, while in the background Winston appeared, traipsing after the phony ghost with what looked like a massive butterfly net in hand.

"That's right," Stantz said, sweating into the TV screen. "Ghostbusters! We're back and we're better than ever, with twice the know-how and twice the particle power to deal with all your supernatural elimination needs."

He glanced over his shoulder, where Winston was still trying to catch the "ghost" without messing up the puppet's wires. "Careful, Winston," Stantz called. "He's a mean one."

Stantz faced the screen again. Sweat trickled down his nose. "And to celebrate our grand reopening, we're giving you twice the value with our special half-price 'Welcome Back' service plan."

Venkman expressed exaggerated shock. "Hold on, Ray!" he exclaimed theatrically. "Half price! Have you gone crazy?"

"I guess so, Pete," Stantz replied, wearing a Cheshire cat smile. "Because *that's not all!* Tell them what else we've got, Egon."

Egon's mind apparently went blank for a moment. Rolling his eyes and frowning, attempting to remember the script, he suddenly recalled his line. "You mean the

Ghostbusters hot-beverage thermal mugs and free balloons for the kids?"

Egon held up a mug bearing the Ghostbusters logo and a limp, uninflated balloon. He glanced at the balloon. Darn. He knew he had forgotten something.

Stantz didn't miss a beat. "You bet, Egon. That's *exactly* what I mean."

Stantz walked toward the screen as bold, flashing letters appeared below him. FULLY BONDED——FULLY LICENSED——SE HABLA ESPANOL.

"So," Stantz announced, "don't you wait another minute. Make *your* supernatural problem *our* supernatural problem. Call now, because we're still . . ."

He glanced over his shoulder. All the Ghostbusters faced the screen and pointed to their unseen viewers. ". . . ready to believe *you.*"

An unseen hand clicked off the TV as Regis Philbin appeared, chatting up a thirteen-year-old pop starlet plugging a TV film about Wisenheimer's disease . . . a sickness that afflicts elderly stand-up comedians.

Rudy, the Manhattan Museum of Art's chief security guard, watched the TV set go blank before he returned to his treasured edition of The *New York Post.* On the front page the headline screamed: GHOSTBUSTERS SAVE JUDGE!

His reading was interrupted by the presence of a guest. Peter Venkman faced Rudy. "Excuse me. I'm looking for Dana Barrett."

Rudy glanced at the visitor. "Room 104. The restoration studio."

Rudy's eyes grew wide. "Hey! Dr. Venkman—*World of the Psychic.* I'm a big, big fan. That used to be one of my *two* favorite shows."

Venkman was obviously flattered. "Thanks," he said suavely. "What's the other one?"

"Bass Masters," Rudy replied. "It's a fishing show. Ever see it?"

Venkman backed away from the security desk. "Yeah, it's really great. Caught it when Meryl Streep was a guest. Take it easy."

Venkman stalked off down the hall, coming to a halt in front of the studio. He eased the door open and entered the large room.

At one end of the studio Dana was hard at work, cleaning a valuable Dutch still life. At the other end Janosz still toiled over the terrible painting of Vigo the rotten.

Dana smiled at Venkman. "Oh, hello, Peter. What are you doing here?"

Venkman shrugged. "I thought you might want to knock off early and let me chase you around the park for a while."

Dana laughed softly. "Thanks, sounds delightful, but I'm working."

Venkman studied the painting she was working on. "So this is what you do, huh? You're really good. Is that a paint-by-numbers job?"

"I didn't paint it," Dana said with a laugh. "I'm just cleaning it. It's an original Vermeer. It's worth about ten million dollars."

Venkman squinted at the painting, holding up his thumb in a classical artist's pose. "What a rip-off! You can go to Art World and get these huge sofa-size paintings for about forty-five bucks. And those black-velvet jobs? Can't top them."

He glanced around the studio, taking in the various pieces of artwork assembled.

"I'm sure they're lovely." Dana sighed. "So are you here just to look at art?"

"As a matter of fact," Venkman replied, "I stopped by to talk to you about your case. We think we know what was pulling the buggy. We found tons of this ecto glop under the street. It's pretty potent stuff."

Dana was confused. "But nothing on the street was moving. Why would the buggy move? Why do these things happen to me?"

Venkman was about to answer when Janosz stuck his head between them. "Dana," he said. "Aren't you going to introduce me to your friend?"

Dana blushed slightly. "Oh, I'm sorry. This is Peter Venkman. Peter, Janosz Poha."

Venkman warily shook Janosz's hand. It felt like grabbing a dead trout. Venkman tried to size Janosz up. Bela Lugosi material in a size petite, he concluded. Janosz avoided Venkman's gaze.

"Pleasure to meet you," he said, staring at his shoes. "I've seen you on television. Not here on business, I hope."

Venkman disengaged his hand. "Naaah. I'm trying to unload all my Picassos, but Dana's not buying."

Venkman looked up and spotted the portrait of Vigo. "What's that you're working on, Johnny?"

Janosz winced at the nickname but let it go. Venkman strolled toward the towering portrait of Vigo, Dana in tow. Janosz sprinted to his post in front of the painting and stood before it, as if on guard duty.

"It's a painting I'm restoring for the new Byzantine exhibition," he blurted. "It's a self-portrait by Prince Vigo the Carpathian. He ruled most of Carpathia and Moldavia in the seventeenth century."

"Too bad for the Moldavians," Venkman concluded, sizing up the painting. Vigo looked like one of the bad guys on a Saturday night wrestling special but with better tights.

"He was a very powerful magician," Janosz said, coming to Vigo's defense. "A genius in many ways and quite a skilled painter."

Venkman made an O shape with his mouth.

"He was also a lunatic and a genocidal madman," Dana pointed out. "I hate this painting. I've felt very uncomfortable since they brought it up from storage."

Venkman understood. "Yeah, It's not exactly the kind of thing you'd want to hang up in the rec room. You know what it needs?"

Venkman grinned and picked up one of Janosz's brushes. "A fluffly little white kitten in the corner."

Venkman made a move for the Vigo portrait. Janosz quickly lunged and snatched the brush away from Venkman, smiling nervously. "We don't go around altering valuable paintings, Dr. Venkman."

"Well, I'd make an exception in this case if I were you." He turned to Dana for support. She frowned at him. Venkman was defeated. He patted Janosz on the back. "I'll let you get back to it. Nice meeting you."

"My pleasure," the thin artist replied.

Venkman walked Dana back to her work space. "Interesting guy," he muttered. "Must be a lot of fun to work with."

"He's very good at what he does," she said.

"I may be wrong, but I think you've got a little crush on that guy."

Dana shook her head. "You're a very sick man."

"That's a given," Venkman said, arching an eyebrow. A beeper attached to his belt started wailing. "Uh-oh," Venkman said. "Gotta go to work. I'll call you."

Venkman headed for the door, calling over his shoulder. "Catch you later, Johnny."

Paintbrush in hand, Vigo towering above him, Janosz winced at the thought of his European name being so crassly Americanized.

Soon the world would know him *and* his name.

15

The garage door to the Ghostbusters' fire-house headquarters rumbled upward, and the team's newly purchased and refurbished ambulance, the Ecto1A, zoomed onto the street. Its ghostly siren moaned and wailed as Winston, in the front seat, went over a laundry list of the day's assignments.

He smiled to himself.

A full day's work.

And not one of the assignments involved kids covered with birthday cake or ice cream.

Diminutive Louis, left out of the action, stood sadly in the garage bay, watching the ambulance disappear. He allowed the garage door to close and was about to return to his office when he began sniffing the air.

There was an odor present. The type of odor he hadn't encountered since some kid passed off a bar of Ex-Lax as Hershey's chocolate to Louis in grade school.

"Oh, jeez," Louis sniffed. "Smells like somebody took a really big—"

Louis froze. Hovering before him was a spud-shaped

green ghost, its pipestick arms flailing away, gleefully chomping down the bag of lunch Louis had brought with him that day. Louis recognized the creature as one of the first trapped by the Ghostbusters years earlier . . . the Slimer.

Slimer, unaware of Louis's presence, glanced downward as Louis glanced upward.

Both Slimer and Louis let out bloodcurdling yells and ran in opposite directions. Slimer was the better for it. He disappeared through a wall. Louis collided with the firehouse's brick wall and knocked himself more senseless than usual. "Help!" he screamed to no one in particular. "There's a *thing*!"

Louis ran out of the room, knowing full well that Slimer would be back for more food and that Louis had just lost at least three perfectly good Twinkies to an apparition.

New Yorkers have a habit of running. They run for subways. They run for cabs. They run from muggers. At the Reservoir in Central Park, however, they run to stay in shape . . . even if it kills them.

On this bright winter's day a gaggle of joggers, of both sexes and all ages, trotted dutifully around the track encircling the Reservoir. They huffed and they puffed, determined to take off the poundage put on during the recent Thanksgiving holiday and to prepare themselves for the edible tonnage they'd consume during the impending Christmas season.

Eventually, it seemed, they all got into step, so that their feet pounded the track in a synchronized manner.

Thump. Thump. Thump.

From behind them, however, came a new sound. Someone was running twice as fast as any jogger present. Someone was going to pass them, and soon.

The last jogger in the pack glanced over her shoulder and let out a bloodcurdling scream.

Gaining on the pack was a strange, skeletal runner, obviously long dead.

The determined spirit sprinted onward, his body encased by a strange, shimmering aura of ethereal light.

Hearing the commotion, the other joggers in the pack turned their heads as the ghostly runner jogged into their midst. The joggers screamed and panicked. Some stumbled and fell onto the track as the spirited spirit strode ever onward.

Other joggers leapt off the track and ran deep into the park at a speed rivaling that of the Concorde, screeching their heads off.

The ghostly jogger didn't seem to notice.

Still running at a steady speed, he raised two bony fingers to his skeletal neck and glanced at his cobweb-encased watch, cautiously checking his long-gone pulse.

A half mile in front of the striding spirit, Venkman and Stantz sat calmly on two benches situated across from one another. The jogging track was sprawled directly in front of them both. Venkman read a particularly scintillating edition of the *New York Post* while dunking a greasy doughnut into a Styrofoam cup filled with coffee.

Across the track, Stantz affected the attitude of Mr. Casual, calmly surveying the jogging track.

Within seconds he saw a lone jogger approaching.

Just your typical, dead-as-a-doornail New York runner surrounded by an unearthly glow.

Stantz cleared his throat.

Across the track, Venkman nodded and continued analyzing the latest installment of *Hagar, the Horrible*.

The ghostly jogger picked up speed.

He barreled down the stretch of track that ran directly between Stantz and Venkman.

As the spirit sprinter passed their benches, Stantz and Venkman simultaneously smashed their feet down on concealed foot switches.

A ghost trap they had previously buried a quarter inch below the dirt jogging track sprang open. The ghost jogger emitted a tiny whimper as the trap caught him full blast, catching him in a shimmering, inverted triangle of light and energy.

The ghostly jogger froze in mid-step, glancing around him. He felt the power of the ghost trap slowly draw him farther and farther down toward the earth.

Within seconds the ghostly jogger was gone.

Trapped.

Stantz slowly got to his feet. Venkman, still pondering the joke in today's *Hagar,* swallowed his doughnut and joined Stantz in closing the rectangular ghost trap.

Stantz held up the glowing trap. Venkman checked his watch. "Do you know that he ran that last lap in under six minutes?" he said.

"Yeah," Stantz agreed. "If he wasn't dead, he'd be an Olympic prospect."

Stantz guided the screaming Ecto1A up in front of the towering World Trade Center, near Manhattan's Wall Street. Venkman, riding shotgun, gazed up at the buildings looming above him and smiled. Big money, he thought.

Winston and Spengler climbed out of the back of the ambulance, carrying their basic monitoring devices.

Stantz made a move for one of the proton packs. Venkman waved him off. He didn't think they'd need any heavy combat equipment.

The four jumpsuited men entered the building.

An anxious Dana Barrett (Sigourney Weaver) rushes to make sure little Oscar is unhurt after his wild carriage ride.

Egon Spengler (Harold Ramis), Ray Stantz (Dan Aykroyd), and Peter Venkman (Bill Murray) take readings over the spot where the baby carriage stopped.

Dana wishes Venkman luck before the trial. He and the others will need it with Louis Tully (Rick Moranis, left) as their lawyer.

The judge, the Ghostbusters, and Tully take cover when the ghosts of the Scoleri brothers make a terrifying appearance in the courtroom.

Now with Winston (Ernie Hudson) on board, the Ghostbus-
ers are back in business. *Above,* they film a new TV commer-
ial. *Below,* the newly refurbished Ectomobile, the Ecto 1A,
its the streets.

Venkman and Stantz clock the speed of a ghostly runner.

"Merry Christmas!" The Ghostbusters clear a store of ghosts in time for the holidays.

Louis Tully prepares to take on Slimer.

Jamie Melnitz (Annie Potts) gets to know Louis a little better.

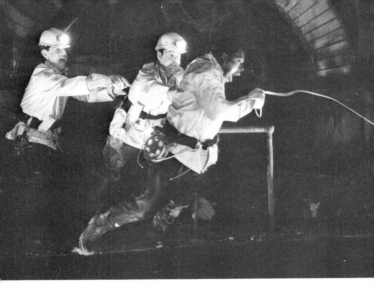

Deep below the streets of New York, Stantz and Spengler try to save Winston as he is pulled into a river of slime.

Covered in the mood-altering goo, the trio is filled with hateful feelings and starts to fight.

Dana tries to save Oscar as he heads for a ghostly nanny in the sky.

The Ghostbusters prepare to blast the slime-encrusted Manhattan Museum of Art, but it will take more power than their proton packs can muster. This job will require the help of all the people of New York.

After being blasted by the Ghostbusters' slime blowers, the painting of Vigo the Carpathian *(above)* melts to reveal a very different scene *(below)*.

Moments later they were ushered into the ornate office of Ed Petrosius, a short, sweating, super-successful and very tightly wound bond salesman.

Petrosius gaped at the Ghostbusters as they marched into his office. He was in the middle of a phone conversation but he clearly wasn't pleased at seeing the quartet in full ghostbusting regalia. He placed a hand over the mouthpiece of the phone.

"What is this?" he hissed. "I'm trying to keep this quiet. Couldn't you put on a coat and tie? You look like janitors."

Venkman glanced at Stantz. They both nodded. Pinhead, they concluded. Rich, spoiled pinhead.

Petrosius barked into the phone, "I'll call you back, Ned. Watch Southern Gulf. If it goes past eight, start buying. Later."

He slammed down the phone and swiveled his chair to face the four Ghostbusters.

"All right," he said impatiently. "How long is this going to take, and what's it going to cost me?"

Venkman offered him a sincere insincere smile. "Well, it depends. Generally we charge an arm and a leg."

Petrosius punched a button on his desktop with a closed fist. His office door automatically slammed shut.

"Look, I got a lot to do and I can't afford to waste a lot of time on this, so don't jerk me around."

Stantz tried the reassuring tack. "Why don't you just tell us what the problem is."

Petrosius stared at his hands.

"Puh-leeeze?" Venkman said, wheedling.

"All right," Petrosius muttered. "Sometimes, every once in a while, things just sort of—well, they just . . . they just kind of *burst into flames*."

He looked up at the Ghostbusters. "You know what I mean?"

Venkman nodded scientifically. "Sure. Things just kind of burst into flames."

"Yeah, you know," Petrosius continued. "Like, I'll be working or talking on the phone and the top of my desk will just catch on fire. You've heard of that, haven't you?"

Venkman rubbed his chin. "Oh, yeah, happens all the time."

"You have a lot of paper around," Stantz offered. "It could be simple spontaneous combustion."

Spengler furrowed his thick brows. "Or it may be *pyrogenesis*."

Petrosius was baffled. "Pyrowhatsis?"

Spengler adjusted his glasses. "Pyrogenesis is the ability some people have to generate great amounts of heat."

Before Petrosius could take that in, the phone on his desk buzzed. "Damn," he muttered, yanking the phone up to his ear. "Yeah? What?"

His eyes grew large. "What are you talking about? I worked the whole thing out with Bill! Forget that crap! Tell Donald to talk to Mike. He okayed the whole thing. And now, one word from Donald and he wants out? No way. We have a deal! Oh, really? My lawyer is an ex-Green Beret!"

He picked up a contract from his desk and began waving it in the air.

Spengler slowly lifted the small, ebony Giga meter and scanned Petrosius while he screamed into the phone.

"No, Bob," Petrosius said, boiling. "*You* eat it! You want to come over here and make me? Anytime, you lying sack of—"

To the right of Petrosius's desk, a wastepaper basket suddenly exploded into flame.

The Ghostbusters exchanged startled looks.

Petrosius glanced at the smoking wastebasket. "Damn it!"

The contract in his hand began to smolder and smoke. He dropped it onto the desktop. It, too, burst into spirals of orange and yellow. Tongues of flame shot forth from the in and out boxes on his desk. And the desk calendar. And the blotter.

Venkman watched more and more of Petrosius's world explode. "Whew! Somebody get the burgers and weenies. This guy is incredible."

Venkman reached over the desk and grabbed a pitcher of water. He tossed it into Petrosius's steaming face. Winston ran to the corner and yanked the inverted plastic bottle from the watercooler. He rushed back to the desk and doused the fire in the wastebasket.

Petrosius watched the water drip from his face and cascade down onto his clothing. He glared at Venkman. "This is a twelve-hundred-dollar suit!" he bellowed.

At that point the curtains behind him caught fire.

Stantz marched bravely up to Petrosius. "I hate to do this, sir," he announced, "but you are a public fire hazard."

Ray Stantz cocked his left arm back and threw a haymaker that caught Petrosius squarely on the jaw. The yammering businessman pitched back into his swivel chair. His chin dropped to his chest.

"Out cold," Winston noted.

"Good policy, Ray," Venkman said, staring at the unconscious man. "From now on let's beat up *all* our customers."

The curtains behind the desk continued to burn, the tongues of flame licking upward. High above the room, the automatic sprinkler system suddenly kicked into action.

The entire office was caught in a machine-made downpour.

Undeterred, a cogitating Spengler walked over to the watercooler. He stuck his hand into the open top and found that the interior sides of the cooler were coated with psycho-reactive slime.

"Interesting," he said.

He glanced at his three companions. They were lifting Petrosius out of his chair.

They carried the unconscious man out of his office and into the reception area like a sack of wet laundry.

Venkman paused momentarily before Petrosius's shocked secretary. "I think Ed's going to be taking some time off."

The Ecto1A pulled up in front of the high-priced store on New York's Fifth Avenue.

A crowd of people was gathered in front of the store's window gazing inside, dumbfounded.

The Ghostbusters jogged up to the locked front door. "Ghostbusters," Winston announced.

The small, frightened manager of the store let them in immediately.

The four Ghostbusters gazed at the strange sight before them.

The high-priced shop sold mostly precious glass. At this moment all the expensive pieces of crystal were floating in the air, several feet above the glass shelves and display tables that had once supported their weight. Stantz and Venkman walked up to the worried, mousy manager while Winston and Spengler set up their small battery of electronic devices in each corner of the room.

Stantz, after studying the phenomenon, turned to the manager. "It's just a straight polarity reversal."

"It is?" The manager blinked.

"Some kind of major PKE storm must have blown through here and affected the silicon molecules in the glass," Stantz continued. He offered the manager a smile and a friendly nod of his groundhog hairdoed head. "We'll have it fixed in a jiff."

"Ready, boys?" he called.

"Ready," Spengler and Winston replied.

"Okay," Stantz commanded. *"Activate!"*

Spengler and Winston simultaneously threw the switches that operated the electronic reversal machines located around the store. A myriad of laserlike beams emerged from the gizmos and engulfed the perimeters of the room, crackling, snapping, and buzzing.

The floating crystal began to shimmy and shake.

The manager of the store watched, horrified, as all the glassware suddenly dropped out of the air. The valuable crystal pieces smashed through the glass shelves and splintered all the display tables. In a moment there was nothing to be seen in the store but tiny shards of sparkling glass.

Spengler and Winston switched off their machines.

Stantz faced the manager with a smile. "See?"

The manager emitted a low moan.

Stantz put a bearlike arm around the tiny man. "So, will that be cash or check?"

The four Ghostbusters emerged from the store to the sound of cheering from the assembled crowd.

From inside the store came an anguished howl.

The crowd froze and turned.

Was it a spirit? A strange and dangerous apparition?

They peered through the window.

No, it was just the weeping manager armed with a straw broom and a dustpan.

Back at Ghostbusting headquarters, would-be spook-chaser Louis lurked surreptitiously behind a pillar leading to the office area, a ghost-trapping pedal near his feet.

Hanging suspended from a string above his desk were several pieces of Kentucky Fried Chicken.

Louis would rid the Ghostbusters of the apparition. He knew he could do it. He had the stamina, the gusto, the intellect. Well, at least the stamina and the gusto.

Louis held his breath as the green Slimer emerged from behind a wall, furtively sniffing the air. Slimer spotted the chicken, cackled, and flew directly toward it.

"Gotcha!" Louis squeaked, slamming his foot down on the foot pedal.

The ghost-trapper popped open and shot a powerful cone of light up toward the ceiling. Slimer munched the chicken calmly as the ghost-trapping rays shot harmlessly by him. What the rays did ensnare was a big chunk of the ceiling, which promptly came crashing down at Louis's feet.

"Uh-oh," Louis moaned.

"Burp," Slimer commented.

Louis slunk out of the room, dejected. On his salary he could never afford the repairs.

He'd do the right thing when the Ghostbusters returned. He'd explain how the ceiling caved in.

He'd lie.

16

Peter Venkman and Winston Zeddemore entered the firehouse's living quarters, exhausted after a tough job. They'd had to trap the spirit of a long-dead game-show host who was inhabiting the set of a TV soap opera. It was a fairly frightening experience for the actors involved. Every time they opened a door on any of their sets, a new prize materialized. The young male lead had nearly ruptured himself when he'd darted out a living-room door and crashed into a brand-new Amana freezer—"with an automatic ice maker," a ghostly voice had intoned as paramedics arrived on the scene.

Venkman fell over onto a sofa. "This pace is too much," he said, moaning. "I'm just going to take a little nap. Wake me on Wednesday."

"Today's Monday," Winston said with a sigh.

"I know that," Venkman replied, his eyes fluttering.

Stantz walked over to the horizontal forms of Winston and Venkman, beaming proudly. "Before you guys pass out, come over here. Spengler and I have something *really* amazing to show you."

"It's not that thing you do with your nostrils, is it?" Venkman said.

Stantz scurried off to the refrigerator. He opened up the freezer and, pushing aside an avalanche of TV dinners and frozen pizza, pulled out a specimen of slime housed in a Tupperware container.

Stantz trotted over to a barely conscious Venkman. "We've been studying the stuff that we took from the subway tunnel."

He ran over to the fire station's microwave oven and popped the container inside. He allowed it to thaw for a moment.

"What are you going to do, eat it?" Venkman groused.

"No," Stantz said. "I'm just restoring it to its normal state."

Winston and Venkman slowly sat up in their chairs. Stantz took the specimen out of the microwave and moved over to a table. He carefully poured a few drops of the ooze into a large petri dish.

Stantz winked at Venkman and Winston. "Now watch *this.*"

He leaned over the dish of slime and began to shout at it. "You worthless piece of *slime*!" he bellowed in mock anger.

Venkman watched in awe as the slime in the dish began to twitch and glow.

Stantz took another deep breath and screamed, "You *ignorant, disgusting blob*!"

The small specimen of ooze began to bubble and swell. Every time Stantz yelled at it, the mess changed its color and slowly began to grow in size.

"I've seen some real *crud* in my life," Stantz continued screaming, "but you're a *chemical disgrace*!"

The specimen suddenly doubled its size and started to spill over the rim of the petri dish. Egon Spengler smiled thinly in a corner of the room. Stantz turned to him. "Okay, Egon, I think that's enough for the day. Let's calm it down."

Spengler picked up an acoustic guitar, slung it over his shoulder, and padded softly up to the petri dish. He nodded at Stantz. Stantz nodded in return. Spengler strummed an opening chord, and then the two Ghost-busters began to serenade the slime.

"Kumbaya, my Lord," they warbled. "Kumbaya."

Venkman and Winston watched the impromptu hootenanny wide-eyed.

As Spengler and Stantz continued to play and sing, the slime stopped bubbling. Slowly but noticeably, the ooze began to calm down and actually shrink.

Stantz and Spengler ended their tune with a flour-ish. Stantz turned to Venkman. Venkman screwed up his face into the fleshy equivalent of a question mark.

"*This* is what you do with your spare time?"

Stantz excitedly pointed to the ooze. "This is an incredible breakthrough, Venkman. Don't you see? We have here a psycho-reactive substance! Whatever that stuff is, it clearly responds to *human* emotional states!"

Spengler nodded. "And we've found it at every event site we've been to lately."

Venkman leapt to his feet. "Mood slime. Now *there* is a major Christmas-gift item."

Stantz motioned for Venkman to be seated. "No way. That would be like giving someone a live hand grenade. This stuff is dangerous. I'm telling you, Pete, based on what we've already seen, we could be facing a major paranormal upheaval."

Winston stared at the slime. "You mean, this stuff actually feeds on *bad vibes*?"

"Like a goat on garbage," Stantz said.

"I love it when you talk science terms," Venkman said, sacking out on the couch.

17

A baleful moon peeked through the starlit skylight above the restoration studio in the near-deserted museum as Dana Barrett cleaned off the last of her brushes and began to put away her supplies. She was bone-tired. It had been a busy day. On the plus side, she had managed to clean a small Renaissance painting. That wasn't bad for a day's work.

Across the studio, the mighty head of Vigo of Carpathia shimmered to life. His eyes lit up as he watched Dana walk past his oil-colored feet.

Dana stopped in her tracks. Someone was watching her. She *felt* it. Yet there was no one else in the studio. She glanced up curiously at the titanic portrait of Vigo. A chill crept through her. She was just being silly, she concluded, and continued to walk toward the exit.

Vigo's thick neck pulsed to life, allowing his head to follow her toward the door.

Dana spun around and caught the movement of the one-dimensional piece of art.

Tensing, she edged back toward the exit door and scrambled through it, slamming it securely behind her.

She nearly ran out of the museum. It would be good to be home with little Oscar, safe and secure in her apartment.

Within two hours Dana had chalked up the entire incident to her nerves. She had been on edge since the baby buggy had gotten away from her. Long hours. Seeing Venkman again. The last two weeks had been a whirlpool of conflicting feelings.

She cradled a cooing Oscar in her arms and carried him into the bathroom. She lowered her child into his bassinet, and wrapping her bathrobe around her nightgown, she bent over the old claw-foot bathtub and turned on the tap.

"Bath time," she called over her shoulder to Oscar.

The water gushed out of the faucet and into the tub. Dana carefully stuck her wrist under the stream of water, checking its temperature. She then turned to Oscar and, bending over the bassinet, began to undress her child.

"Look at you." She smiled adoringly. "I think we got more food on your shirt than we got in your mouth."

The baby clapped appreciatively at his mother's wit.

Behind Dana, the water gushing from the faucet slowly changed into shining, shimmering slime. The slime hit the gathered water in the tub with a resounding plop and settled itself at the very bottom of the tub. Both of the spigots on the tub began to spin wildly as more and more slime burrowed beneath the surface of the water.

Dana, unaware of the change in the tub's attitude,

routinely reached over to a shelf and squirted a stream of bubble bath into the water.

She returned her attention to Oscar. The rim of the tub puckered up like a clamshell and its sides convulsed as the newly animated piece of porcelain sucked up the bubble bath.

Belch.

Dana proudly picked up her beautiful baby boy out of his bassinet and held him above the tub.

"Bathies," she cooed.

She lowered Oscar toward the waiting tub. Without warning the tub began to shimmy and shake before her, its sides rising up like a gigantic, snapping clamshell, poised to snap up the boy and drag it down to the awaiting layer of glop.

Dana screamed and raised her baby.

The bathtub snapped at her.

Dana clutched Oscar to her chest and slowly backed away from the convulsing tub. Creak. Creak. Creak. The tub's stumpy legs slowly began to creep across the tile floor toward Dana.

Dana turned and ran out of the bathroom.

The tub made an attempt to dash after her but found the doorway too narrow a passageway to clear.

The tub growled in anger, vomiting up buckets of creeping, crawling slime.

Dana dashed through her apartment. She grabbed her keys and headed for the front door. She had to find a safe place to hide. A place no spirit would *dare* invade.

Peter Venkman lay sprawled upon the floor of his apartment, sound asleep. He was still fully clothed and had not quite made it into his bedroom, nodding out some three feet away from its entranceway.

Venkman's loft apartment resembled the site of a

recent spate of tornadoes. Tattered, mismatched pieces of furniture were covered with old magazines, books, newspapers, videotapes, and a few very ripe pieces of half-eaten pizza.

Venkman's eyes fluttered as his front doorbell chimed.

He slowly got to his feet, and trying carefully not to step on any debris that would either break under his weight or stick to his shoes, he zigzagged sleepily to the door.

He eased the door open.

Outside stood Dana, wearing her short nightgown under an overcoat. Baby Oscar was in her arms, naked but for a baby blanket hastily wrapped around him.

"I'm s-sorry," Dana stammered. "Were you on your way out?"

Venkman looked down and saw that he still had on his coat, scarf, and hat. "No. I just got in . . . a couple of hours ago. Come on in."

Dana entered the messy apartment. Venkman gazed at her nightgown. "Are we having a pajama party?"

"Peter," Dana blurted, "my bathtub tried to eat Oscar!"

Venkman stared at Dana. So young. So beautiful. Possibly so nuts. He thought a moment. "You know, if anyone else told me that, I'd have serious doubts. But coming from you, I can't honestly say I'm surprised."

"I must be losing my mind," Dana said, near tears. "At the museum today I could have sworn that terrible painting of Vigo *moved* and looked right at me!"

"Who could blame him?" Venkman shrugged. "Were you wearing this nightgown?"

"I don't know what to do anymore," she said with a moan.

"I'll get Ray and Egon to check out the bathtub. You better stay here."

Venkman trotted off to his bedroom. Dana glanced around the loft. She was amazed at the disorder. It looked like Hiroshima after the A-bomb blast. Venkman jogged back into the room, carrying an old football sweatshirt. He gently lifted Oscar from Dana's arms. The baby's blanket fell away.

"Now this kid has a *serious* nudity problem," he surmised.

He spread the sweatshirt out on the sofa, placed Oscar on it, and began tying it around the child like a diaper.

"This is Joe Namath's old number, you know," he informed the baby. "You could get a lot of chicks with this. Just don't pee in it."

Dana stood, trembling. "Peter, what about the *bathtub*?"

"We'll take care of that," he said, reaching for a phone and dialing. "Ray? Pete. Listen. Get over to Dana's right away. Her bathtub pulled a fast one. Tried to eat her kid."

"It was full of this awful pink ooze," Dana offered.

Venkman nodded, still cradling the phone. "Sounds like another slime job, Ray. No, they're both all right. They're here now. Right. Let me know."

Venkman hung up the phone. "They're going over there right now. You might as well make yourself at home. Let me show you around."

He carefully walked into the kitchen area. "This is the *cuisine de maison,*" he announced.

The kitchen looked worse than the living room. The sink boasted a mountain range of dirty dishes, and the counters were stacked with all sorts of rotted food and crunched TV-dinner boxes. Venkman smiled suavely and pulled a colossal trash bag from a drawer. He tossed it onto the floor and started stiff-arming trash off the counter into it.

He glanced at the junk-coated dishes in the sink. "Umm. We may have to wash some of these if you get hungry."

He stumbled toward the refrigerator and eased open the door. A horrible stench emerged. He slammed the door shut. "But . . . there's no real food, anyway, so forget about it. I have all kinds of carryout menus if you feel like ordering."

He yanked open a cabinet drawer. Inside were at least a hundred dog-eared menus. There was everything from Chinese and Mexican cuisine to a flyer from Mr. Nut's International House of Peanut Butter and Jelly.

He strode across the loft to a door. "And the bathroom's right here," he said with a flourish. "Uh, let me just tidy up a few things."

Dana smiled. "Peter, this is very nice, but you don't have to do any of this, you know."

Venkman grinned gallantly and, slinging another trash bag over his shoulder, dashed inside. A toilet flushed. The shower ran. The sound of glass, tin, and wood could be heard tumbling into the trash bag.

Within a minute Venkman emerged, carrying a full trash bag over his shoulder. "The shower works but it's a little tricky," he advised. "Both spigots are marked 'hot.' It takes a little practice, but at least this one won't try to eat you."

Dana began to ease herself onto Venkman's ratty sofa. Venkman walked by her, the trash slung over his shoulder. "Be careful on that sofa, though. It's a butt biter."

Dana nearly leapt to her feet.

"But the bed's good." Venkman smiled. "And I just

changed the sheets, so if you get tired, feel free. In fact, I think you should *definitely* plan on spending the night here."

Dana offered him a crooked grin. "Really? And how would we handle the sleeping arrangements?"

Venkman dropped the second trash bag in the kitchen and pondered the problem. "Hmm. For me, it's best if I sleep on my side and you spoon up right behind me with your arms around me. If we go the other way, I'm afraid your hair will be getting in my face all night."

Dana stared at Venkman. "How about you on the sofa and me in bed with the baby?"

Venkman nodded. "Or we could do that."

"Thank you," Dana said, picking up Oscar. She cradled the baby in her arms. "Poor baby. I think I should put him down now."

Venkman walked up to them both. "I'll put him down for you."

He stared at the child. "You are way too short! And your belly button sticks out! And you're nothing but a burden to your poor mother!"

He picked up the giggling baby and carried Oscar into the bedroom.

Dana watched Venkman play daddy, and smiled.

For the first time in ages she felt relaxed.

And safe.

Very, very safe.

She savored the feeling, sensing that it wouldn't last for very long.

18

Peter Venkman paced back and forth in front of the Manhattan Museum of Art, watching the building's first horde of art lovers make their way up the front stairs toward the entrance.

He checked his watch.

The Ecto1A screeched to a halt in front of the curb. Stantz, Spengler, and Winston scrambled out, Winston muttering under his breath about crosstown traffic.

Venkman, clearly concerned, cornered Stantz. "Did you find anything at Dana's apartment?"

Stantz shrugged. "Nothing. Just some mood-slime residue in and around the bathtub."

"But we did pay an interesting visit to Ray's bookstore this morning," Winston said, grinning.

Venkman rolled his eyes. There was *nothing* interesting in Ray's bookstore if you didn't count the cockroaches.

Stantz smiled and whipped a small, dog-eared volume out of Ecto1A. "We turned up some intriguing stuff on this Vigo character you mentioned."

He held up the book. It was nearly falling apart. "I found the name Vigo the Carpathian in Leon Zundinger's *Magicians, Martyrs, and Madmen*. Listen to this! Egon?"

Spengler held up a photocopy or two taken from the crumbling book. " 'Vigo the Carpathian, born 1505, died 1610—' "

Venkman blinked. "A hundred and five years old? He really hung on, didn't he?"

Stantz smiled knowingly. "And he didn't die of old age, either. He was poisoned, stabbed, shot, hung, stretched, disemboweled, and drawn and quartered."

"I guess he wasn't too popular at the end there," Winston theorized.

"No," Spengler agreed. "He wasn't exactly a man of the people."

He began reading again. " 'Also known as Vigo the Cruel, Vigo the Torturer, Vigo the Despised, and Vigo the Unholy.' "

"This guy was a bad monkey," Stantz explained. "He dabbled in all the black arts. And listen to this prophecy: Just before his head died, his last words were: 'Death is but a door, time is but a window. *I'll be back!* ' "

Venkman wasn't impressed. "That's *it*? That's all he said? 'I'll be back'?"

Spengler shrugged. "Uh, it's a rough translation from the Moldavian."

Venkman sighed. "Okay. Let's visit Viggy."

The Ghostbusters picked up their paranormal monitoring equipment and walked up the front steps toward the museum.

Dressed in full gear, they marched through the lobby. Rudy, the security guard, stared at them in disbelief. Venkman was in the lead.

"Hey, Dr. Venkman," Rudy asked with a smile, "what's going on?"

"We're just going back to the restoration studio for a minute," Venkman replied.

Rudy frowned. "Oh, I can't let you do that. Mr. Poha left strict orders. He told me not to let you back there anymore."

Venkman stiffened. His eyebrows knitted together. He glared at Rudy in ultra mock seriousness. "Okay," he said confidentially. "We were trying to keep this quiet, but I think *you* can be trusted. Tell him, Ray."

Stantz walked up to Rudy and in a clipped tone announced, "Mister, you have an ecto-paritic, subfusionary flux in this building."

Rudy was aghast, although he wasn't quite sure why. "We got a *flux?*"

Winston strode forward. "Man, you got a flux and a *half.*"

Rudy looked to Venkman. Venkman glanced at Stantz. Rudy shifted his gaze to Stantz. Stantz nodded grimly, raising his left hand. He began counting fingers. "Now, if you don't want to be the—one two three four—*fifth* person ever to die in meta-shock from a planar rift, I suggest you get down from behind that desk and don't move until we give you the signal, 'Stabilized—all clear.' "

Rudy nodded and swallowed hard. He slowly slithered out of his chair and crouched down behind his desk, and the Ghostbusters marched back toward the restoration studio.

Inside the studio, Janosz was patiently working on the horrible portrait of Vigo the Lowlife when the Ghostbusters barged through the door. Janosz hastily tossed down his paints and brushes and rushed over to the door in an attempt to bar their entry.

"Dr. Venkman?" he blurted. "Uhh, Dana is not here."

Venkman flashed him a cool smile. "I know."

Janosz was sweating now. "Then why have you come?"

Venkman pushed the agitated artist aside. "We've got a major creep alert, and we're just going down the list. Your name was first."

Janosz stood, quivering in terror. Stantz turned to Winston and Spengler. "Let's sweep the area, boys."

The three Ghostbusters pulled out their hand-held monitoring devices and began to stroll through the studio area. Janosz was growing more and more nervous. Venkman sidled up to him.

"You know," he said, "I never got to ask you: Where are you from, Johnny?"

Janosz mind reeled. "Uh, the Upper West Side."

Spengler glanced at his PKE meter. "This entire room is extremely hot, Peter."

Janosz turned to Venkman. "What exactly are you looking for?"

Venkman offered him a totally insincere, reassuring smile. "We'll know it when we find it. You just sit tight, Johnny. This won't take long."

Stantz pulled out the shoebox-shaped Giga meter. It began to click in his hand. The needle began to quiver and quake, eventually sliding to the extreme right-hand side of the small screen. Stantz looked up. Inadvertently he had aimed the Giga meter directly at the Brobding-nagian-sized portrait of Vigo the louse. Venkman joined Stantz.

He looked up at the painting of the fierce warrior. "This is the one that made ga-ga eyes at Dana."

Venkman walked up to the portrait. He stared up into Vigo's dull eyes. "Hey, *you*!" he called. "Viggy! Look at me! Down here! I'm talking to you, stud! Hey! Look at me when I'm talking to you!"

Stantz and Venkman watched the painting for any sign of movement.

On the canvas Vigo's eyes remained motionless, focused lifelessly on something far off in the distance.

Stantz sighed. Venkman's tactics weren't working. Venkman, however, refused to give up. He whipped out a small camera and began darting to and fro at the base of the painting, snapping away.

"Beautiful, beautiful, Viggy. That's it. Work with me, baby. Just have fun with it."

Venkman snapped away. After a full roll was used, he stopped his photography riff and turned to Stantz. "Okay, so he's playing it cool." Venkman shrugged. "Let's finish up and get the heck out of here."

Stantz nodded. "I'll get one more reading."

Venkman walked off, disgusted. Stantz, left alone in front of the towering painting, scanned the canvas one last time with his Giga meter. He started with the feet and worked his way up the legs to the torso, then aimed the meter at the neck. Finally Stantz found himself gazing at the face of Vigo.

Vigo's eyes slowly flickered to life.

Stantz felt his body stiffen.

A fierce red light welled up Vigo's evil eyes.

Stantz felt the power of Vigo enter his eyes and burn itself right down to the depths of his very soul.

Stantz stood before the painting, transfixed. Deep down within him he knew what was happening to him. He knew he should turn away, but the conscious being known as Ray Stantz was gradually fading away, enslaved by a new evil being. Stantz's childlike eyes narrowed to reptilian slits. His open, optimistic face began to grow taut. His lips, capable of a smile at the most dire of occasions, slowly twisted themselves into a terrifying sneer.

Stantz felt an arm on his shoulder.

He blinked.

His body regained fluidity.

"Now that's one *ugly* dude," Winston said to Stantz.

Stantz shook his head. "Huh? What?"

Stantz made a concerted effort to figure out what had happened to him during the last minute or so. Everything was a blank.

"You finished here?" Winston asked.

"What? Huh? Oh, yeah. Sure. Sure," Stantz said, his legs still feeling wobbly.

"Are you all right?" Winston queried. "You coming down with something?"

Stantz managed a feeble smile for his good and loyal friend, Winston. "No, I'm fine. I just got light-headed for a second there. Let's go."

Winston aimed Stantz toward the exit door. "Okay, buddy, but if you feel like calling it an early day, it's okay. I'll pick up the slack."

Stantz nodded woozily. "I appreciate that, Winston. I really do."

The Ghostbusters left the portrait of Vigo and the figure of Janosz Poha behind them.

Janosz turned to the painting of Vigo and smiled.

Soon, he realized, the Ghostbusters would stand in their way no more.

19

The Ghostbusters walked down the museum's front steps toward Ecto1A.

"There's definitely something going on in that studio," Spengler surmised. "The PKE levels were max-plus, and the Giga meter was showing all red."

Winston agreed. "I'd put my money on that Vigo character."

Venkman smirked. "Yeah, *that's* a safe bet."

Venkman and Spengler climbed into the rear of the Ecto1A. Venkman glanced at Stantz before shutting the rear hatch. "You and Spengler see what else you can dig up on Vigo and this little weasel, Poha. Those two were made for each other."

Stantz said nothing. He nodded. He was getting a headache. A bad one.

"Want me to drive?" Winston asked.

"No," Stantz said. "I'm fine."

Stantz slid in behind the wheel. Winston eased himself into the passenger's seat.

A strange smile played across Ray Stantz's face as

he turned the ignition key and slammed his right foot down on the gas, sending the Ecto-2 screeching away from the curb.

Winston gave him a nervous look.

Stantz sent the ambulance skidding and swerving around the streets of Manhattan as he ostensibly headed back for the firehouse. His eyes seemed vacant. His face was devoid of any awareness of the commotion he was causing all around him. Stantz swerved suddenly. He slammed his hand down on the car's horn.

"Idiot!" he shrieked to a passing motorist.

He cut off another car. "Move it, you jerk!" he roared.

Winston glanced into the rear of the Ecto1A, where Venkman and Spengler were being tossed around like rag dolls, along with their ghostbusting equipment.

Stantz began to pick up speed. Thirty-five. Forty. Fifty miles an hour. He roared through red lights, narrowly avoiding pedestrians.

Winston looked at Ray, beads of perspiration dribbling down his forehead. "Going a little fast, aren't we, Ray?"

Stantz glared at Winston. His eyes were deranged, unfeeling. "Are you telling me how to drive?" he asked, sneering.

"No, I just thought—"

"Well, don't think!" Ray bellowed.

He stood on the accelerator, fishtailing in front of a bus and two cars.

In the back of Ecto1A, Venkman and Spengler continued to bounce around.

"I want to talk to our mechanic about these shocks," Venkman muttered, his head slamming into the roof of the auto.

Venkman and Spengler clung to the safety straps above their heads, twirling like aerial stars in a circus.

In the front seat, Winston moved from panic level to out-and-out we're-gonna-die mode. He turned to Stantz. "Are you crazy, man? You're going to kill somebody!"

Stantz emitted a devilish cackle. He turned to Winston and smiled demonically. "Wrong," he announced. "I'm going to kill *everybody*!"

Stantz sent the Ecto1A sailing off the street and headed for a small public park.

He carefully aimed the vehicle for a large tree.

Winston's eyes widened in disbelief as he watched the tree loom larger and larger.

At the last possible moment he reached over and coldcocked Stantz with a strong right hook. Stantz's body went limp. Winston reached over and, yanking the wheel, slid his left foot across the front of the seat and slammed on the brakes.

The car lurched to a halt. It barely grazed the tree.

The four Ghostbusters tumbled out of the car, dazed and shaken but unhurt.

Stantz dropped to all fours, shaking his head. It was as if he were awakening from a deep, long sleep. He staggered to his feet, his senses still swimming. He glanced confusedly at Venkman.

"What happened?"

"You just picked up three penalty points on your driver's license," Venkman informed him.

Stantz gaped at the Ecto1A and the tree. Within seconds Winston was at his side. "Are you all right?"

Stantz nodded, the first flickerings of understanding playing across his face. "Yeah, I guess so. It was the strangest thing. I knew what I was doing but I couldn't stop. This really *terrible feeling* came over me and—I don't know—I just felt like driving into that tree and ending it all. Whew! Sorry, boys."

Venkman turned to Spengler. "Watch him, Egon," he whispered. "Don't even let him shave."

Winston inspected the damage to the car. "No big deal," he said with a sigh. "Just another fender bender in the Big Apple."

Venkman rolled his eyes. Yeah. Right.

20

Venkman and Winston walked into the firehouse, bone-tired after spending most of the morning haggling with an auto mechanic about getting the repairs done on Ecto1A as quickly and as cheaply as possible. The mechanic wasn't too responsive until Venkman threatened to summon up the spirit of the guy's long-dead mother-in-law. Within ninety minutes the Ecto1A looked fine. The mechanic even threw in a tune-up for free.

In the firehouse lab area, Stantz and Spengler were hard at work. Stantz took a small sample of the psycho-reactive slime out of a small container. He had painted a smiley face on the lid to keep the ooze calm.

"What's up?" Winston asked.

"We now know the *negative* potential of this stuff," Stantz announced. "We've isolated this specimen and we're running tests on it to see if we can get an equally strong *positive* reaction."

Venkman was intrigued. "What kind of tests?"

Stantz shuffled about before the container, embarrassed. "Well, we sing to it. We talk to it. We say supportive, nurturing things . . ."

"You're not *sleeping* with this stuff, are you?" Venkman asked in mock horror.

Spengler coughed, reacting as if he *might* be. Venkman and Winston watched intently as Stantz spooned some of the psycho-reactive slime into an old toaster.

"We've mostly been going with the music angle," he said.

"We've identified several songs that seem to have a calming or a mediating effect on the slime," Spengler added.

"We tried all the sappy stuff," Stantz continued. " 'Kumbaya,' 'Everything Is Beautiful,' and 'It's a Small World' all scored high."

Spengler offered a thin smile. "But the song that really goosed its molecules is the 1967 Jackie Wilson hit, 'Higher and Higher.' "

Venkman didn't believe it.

"Watch this." Stantz grinned. He walked over to a boom box and flicked on a tape. The sweet, silky voice of the late, great Jackie Wilson blasted through the room.

The slime-encased toaster began to shake and spin. Winston's jaw dropped open as the toaster actually started to swivel back and forth—in time with the pulsating music. Venkman gaped in astonishment at the bopping toaster as it actually shot two pieces of darkened bread into the air and, swerving on the tabletop, caught them back in its slots without missing a beat.

"I don't care what you say," Venkman said, beaming. "We're going to bottle this stuff and sell it. We'll make a fortune."

Winston was a tad more skeptical. "Right, and the

first time someone gets mad, their toaster will eat their hand."

Venkman wasn't daunted. "Okay. Okay. So we'll put a warning on the label."

Stantz switched off the Jackie Wilson tape and the toaster sputtered to a complete standstill.

"We're investigating the practical applications," Spengler said. "But stocking stuffers isn't one of them. We think it could be a useful tool against certain types of spiritual manifestations."

Venkman didn't get it.

"We have a prototype designed for a pressure-forced, neutronically metered, fully portable delivery system," Stantz announced.

Venkman still didn't get it.

Stantz sighed. "Basically it's a *slime-blower.*"

He held up a bazookalike tube attached to a set of compressed air tanks.

Venkman wasn't overly awed. "Yeah, well keep up the good work. See if you can keep it under a hundred and fifty pounds."

Venkman walked over to the toaster and stuck his fingers in one of the slots.

Venkman sneered at the slime within. "Go ahead, I dare you."

Venkman suddenly screamed, as if the toaster were gnawing the flesh off his fingers. He couldn't remove his hand from the goop-empowered mechanism. The other three Ghostbusters leapt forward to his aid.

Venkman faced them with a smile. "Just kidding," he said, easily removing his hand from the toaster.

With that he left the room, leaving the other three Ghostbusters relieved, but more than slightly p.o.'d, behind him.

After making a quick stop at Dana's deserted apartment, Venkman made his way downtown to his loft. He walked up to the front door, tentatively holding a small bouquet of flowers, as well as one of Dana's small suitcases.

He produced his keys, unlocked the door, and swung it open.

"Honeeeeey," he called. "I'm home!"

He eased the door shut behind him. He gazed in terror at the sight before him. Never in all his years as a Ghostbuster had he witnessed such an appalling sight.

"I knew it!" he muttered. "She *cleaned!*"

The loft was spotless.

The withering leftovers had been removed.

The old newspapers and magazines had been banished.

Books were now neatly stacked on shelves.

The thirteen layers of dust in the kitchen had been washed away.

The hairballs—and Venkman didn't even have *pets*—had been vacuumed from the furniture.

Venkman heard the shower running in the bathroom. Placing the suitcase and the flowers down, he slowly tiptoed to the bathroom. The door was half open. He peeked inside. He could barely make out the form of Dana, clad only in layers of soap, behind the shower curtain.

Sighing, he eased the door closed and moved to the bedroom, where little Oscar lay asleep. Dana had surrounded the tyke with large pillows to prevent him from taking an impromptu swan dive off the bed.

Venkman smiled.

Maybe *this* was what he needed in his life. He slammed the flat of his hand into his forehead. Naaah. This kind of life was for normal people, not Ghostbusting kind of guys.

He spun around and collided with Dana as she exited the bathroom wrapped only in a towel. She quickly darted back inside.

Venkman made a concerted effort not to drool. He had just gotten his shirt cleaned.

Dana reemerged from the bathroom wearing a long terry-cloth robe. Venkman leered at her. "Now, don't tell me you didn't do that on purpose. You're trying to torture me, aren't you?"

Dana regarded him impassively.

"Are you all squeaky clean now?" Venkman asked.

Dana shot him a withering smile. "Yes, I'm very clean. Did they find anything in my apartment?"

Before Venkman could answer, Dana marched past him and entered the bedroom, closing the door in his face.

"Nothing," Venkman shouted through the door. "They stayed there all night, went through your personal stuff, made a bunch of long-distance calls, and cleaned out your refrigerator. That's about it."

Dana opened the door, still wearing the heavy robe. "So what do I do now?"

Venkman grinned. "You get dressed and we go out. I've got a baby-sitter and everything. Trust me, you need it."

Dana was tempted. "You don't have to entertain me, you know."

"I know," Venkman said, trotting into the living room and returning with her suitcase. "I brought some of your clothes."

Dana smiled, took the small suitcase, and eased the bedroom door shut. "Wear something intriguing," Venkman said to the closed door.

He walked down a small corridor and opened his

closet, looking for his good suit. "Did you happen to see some shirts on the floor in here?" he called.

"I put them in your hamper," Dana said from the bedroom. "I thought they were dirty."

Venkman shook his head mournfully. "Next time ask me first, okay? I have more than two grades of laundry. There are lots of subtle levels between *clean* and *dirty.*"

He walked into the misty bathroom and attacked the hamper, yanking out pieces of clothing. Shirts. Slacks. Socks. "Hmm," he muttered, "these aren't so bad yet. You just hang them up for a while and they're fine."

He smelled the armpit of one shirt, frowned, and, reaching into the medicine cabinet, sprayed it for a full minute with deodorant. He sniffed it a second time. Better. Definitely better.

Pouring a healthy splash of after-shave into each sock, Venkman smiled.

He was all set for a night on the town.

21

Janine sat in the reception area of the Ghostbusters' firehouse, working late. Above her, she heard noises coming from the lab area that she knew should have been deserted.

She wasn't alarmed. She realized it would be Louis. Poor Louis, she thought with a sigh. The closest he would ever come to a brainstorm was a slight drizzle. Still, there was something about him that appealed to her.

He *meant* well. Janine supposed what appealed to her about Louis was that he exuded the same type of personality as the pets she'd chosen as a child. While all the other kids picked pedigreed dogs, she'd always gone for the stray mutts. Dogs who were so goofy and out of whack that you didn't expect anything from them. If they gnawed the newspaper instead of carrying it into the house, who could blame them?

She covered her computer and made her way up toward the lab, a warm smile on her elfin face.

Inside the lab, Louis was dressed in a Ghostbusters jumpsuit. It fit him like oversize feety pajamas. He had a proton pack strapped onto his back, but the straps were so loose that the pack banged into his rear end whenever he moved.

"Okay, Stinky," he muttered. "This is it. Showdown time. You and me, pal. You think you're smarter than I am? We'll see about that!"

He faced the ceiling and squeaked. "Oh, hello, Pizza Man! Oh, two larges! I ordered only one. Pepperoni and pineapple, my absolute favorite. I guess *I'll have to eat these both by myself!*"

The green ghost Slimer poked his head down through the ceiling and scanned the room for the grub.

"Okay, let's boogie," Louis whispered.

Louis whirled around and fired a proton stream at Slimer just as Janine entered the room. Slimer retreated easily. Janine gulped and ducked as a ragged bolt of energy streaked across the lab and seared the wall behind her.

Louis stood there, trembling. "Ohmigod!" he shouted. "I'm sorry. I didn't mean to do that. It was an accident."

He flip-flopped across the lab to Janine. The receptionist slowly straightened up. "What are you doing up here?" she asked him.

Louis began to sweat. "I was trying to get that smelly green ghost. The guys asked me to help out. I'm like the fifth Ghostbuster."

Janine smiled at him sweetly. "Why would you want to be a Ghostbuster if you're already an accountant?"

Louis thought hard. "Oh, no. It's not like that. It's just if one of the guys calls in sick or gets hurt."

Louis quickly slipped off the proton pack. The pack slid to the floor, nearly toppling Louis onto his back.

"So," Janine said, "have you made any plans for New Year's Eve?"

Louis shrugged. "No. I celebrate at the beginning of

my corporate tax year, which is March first. That way I beat the crowds."

Janine was impressed. "That's very practical. I hate going out on New Year's Eve too."

Louis and Janine exchanged smiles. Suddenly Louis felt awkward. There was a warmth welling up within him. He was either very attracted to Janine, or else he was experiencing the aftershocks of a Thai food lunch Venkman had talked him into.

"Well," Janine said, turning, "good night, Louis."

Louis stumbled forward, his mouth getting the best of his brain. "Janine, do you feel like maybe getting something to eat on the way home? Have you ever been to Tad's? It's a pretty good deal. You get a steak, baked potato, a roll, and a salad with your choice of dressing for $5.29. You can't beat that!"

Janine faced Louis, bestowing upon him a wide, adoring smile. "I'd like to, Louis, but I told Dr. Venkman I'd baby-sit for his friend."

Louis's face fell instantly. "Oh," he murmured. "Maybe some other time, then."

"Do you want to baby-sit with me?" Janine offered.

Louis brightened. "Oh, *sure*!" he exclaimed. "That sounds *great*!"

Louis trotted up to Janine, and the twosome left the firehouse together.

Downtown, Venkman sat waiting for the baby-sitter in the center of his living room. His recently sprayed suit and socks ensemble looked mighty fine, even if he did have to say so himself.

His front doorbell rang.

He leapt out of the couch and trotted to the door, expecting to welcome Janine.

Instead he gazed upon Stantz, Spengler, and Winston. They stood in the hallway wearing over-the-hip rubberized wading boots, firemen's slickers, and miners' helmets. They each carried several sensing devices, meters, collection jars, and photographic equipment. If Venkman didn't know better, he would have sworn they were heading out on a major *National Geographic* spelunkers' expedition.

Venkman motioned them in. "Don't tell me, let me guess. All-you-can-eat barbecued rib night at the Sizzler?"

"Better!" Stantz beamed. "We're going down into the sewer system to see if we can trace the source of that psycho-reactive slime flow. We thought you might want to come along!"

Venkman snapped his fingers theatrically. "Darn it! I wish I'd have known you were going. I'm stuck with these silly dinner reservations."

Spengler ignored him. "You know, animals and lower life forms often anticipate major disasters. Given the new magnetheric readings, we could see a tremendous breeding surge in the cockroach population."

"Roach breeding?" Venkman replied. "Gosh! This is sounding better and better!"

Venkman called through the closed bedroom door. "Dana? The boys are going down under the sewers tonight to look for slime. Egon thinks there might even be some kind of big roach-breeding surge. Should we forget about dinner and go with them instead?"

Dana emerged from the bedroom looking gorgeous in a long, slinky evening gown, her auburn hair cascading down onto her shoulders.

"Wow!" Stantz concluded.

Dana surveyed the Ghostbusters' grab-bag outfits. "Hi!" she offered meekly.

The Ghostbusters, slightly flustered, nodded and waved back.

Venkman faced Stantz and Spengler. "Ray? Egon? I

think we're going to have to pass on the sewer trip. Let me know what you find out."

He led the Ghostbusters to the door. Stantz heaved a sigh. "Okay, but you're missing out on all the fun."

Venkman eased the door shut behind them.

In the hall, Stantz, Spengler, and Winston passed Janine and Louis in the hall. They smiled at each other.

Louis was awestruck by the professional-looking trio. "Hey!" he exclaimed. "Where are you going?"

The Ghostbusters walked into the elevator without saying a word.

"Okay," Louis said. "Talk to you later."

Janine knocked on Venkman's front door. Louis was impressed with Janine's importance. He had never visited Venkman at home before. In fact, up until now, he hadn't realized Venkman *had* a home.

Venkman swung the door open, clad in his dapper suit and looking very suave.

Louis sniffed the air. It reeked of drugstore cologne, spray-on deodorant, and talcum powder.

"Come in." Venkman smiled.

"I just saw the guys in some nifty outfits," Louis said enthusiastically.

"They were helping change a diaper," Venkman said, leading them into the apartment. "It was a pretty messy one."

Janine looked around the loft, frowning. Even when tidied up, the place resembled nothing more than a clubhouse from the old *Our Gang* comedies. "You actually live here?"

"Yes, Janine, I do," Venkman confessed.

"I think it's *neat*," Louis offered.

Venkman smiled at Janine. "But I'm thinking of moving out soon."

Janine shrugged and, grabbing the TV listings, sat

before the battered television to see if it worked. Louis chatted up Venkman. "I hope you don't mind me being here. I just thought I could keep Janine company."

"It's fine," Venkman said, putting a fatherly arm around the diminutive nerd. "Knock yourself out. But I don't want to come home and find you two making out on the couch!"

"Oh, no." Louis blushed. "We're just good friends."

"Okay, let's keep it that way." Venkman winked, leading Dana out the door.

Hailing a cab, he escorted Dana to one of the swankiest new restaurants in Manhattan: Armand's. It was the kind of restaurant that catered to the very rich and the very blow-dried. Raw fish was served alongside Southwestern cuisine. The wine tasted like Ripple but cost fifty times as much, and the piped-in Muzak sounded like vintage elevator music but was called new age subliminal. Venkman would have preferred a pool hall or an Irish pub, but he figured this was more Dana's style.

The cab pulled to a stop in front of Armand's. Venkman frowned. When he had moved to New York, the place had been a Laundromat. He sighed. He could use a Laundromat right about now.

He guided Dana through the front entrance and slipped the maître d' a five-dollar bill.

"Your best table, Armand," Venkman cooed, feeling like Douglas Fairbanks.

The maître d' peeked at the bill and grimaced. Venkman made sure that Dana missed that, and frowning, whipped out a twenty. He stuffed it into the maître d's hand. The man smiled.

"This better be good," Venkman said to the man.

The maître d' escorted them to a wonderful table. Venkman glanced over his shoulder. The couple next to them had ordered a fish that still had the head attached. A cold eye stared blankly at Venkman.

Jeez, he thought, sitting down. At least they could have put a *smile* on the thing.

He glanced at the menu. His heart sank.

No burgers.

Venkman sighed and made the best of it, ordering caviar and champagne. A slavish waiter brought their appetizer and spirits immediately.

Venkman raised a glass to Dana. "To a wonderful lady. A ninja warrior. A woman who stands tall," he toasted. "It's *your* night."

Dana smiled sadly and raised her glass. "To the most charming, nicest, kindest . . ."

"Why, you're talking about me!" Venkman grinned.

". . . most unusual man I've ever broken up with."

They both sipped their champagne.

"Speaking of breaking up with really neat guys," Venkman said casually. "So, tell me why you *dumped* me."

Dana slid back into her chair. "Oh, Peter. I didn't dump you. I just had to protect myself. You really weren't very good for me, you know."

"Hey," Venkman replied, "*I'm* not even good for me."

"Why do you say things like that?" Dana said. "You're so much better than you know."

"Thank you." Venkman grinned. "If I had that kind of support on a daily basis, I could definitely shape up by the turn of the century."

Dana smiled, her forehead feeling the first buzz of the champagne. "So why don't you call me in the year 2000?"

Venkman leaned over to kiss her. "Let me jingle you right now."

Dana pulled back. "Maybe I should call Janine."

Venkman continued to lean and pucker. "Don't

worry. Janine has a very special way with children. I know. I've seen her."

Venkman's lips touched Dana's. For a split second all the worries and all the pressures of the day faded. For a split second they were together. In love.

Things were not quite as lovely at Venkman's apartment. Janine sat transfixed before the television, watching a particularly engrossing episode of *Jake and the Fatman*.

Louis, meanwhile, paced around the living room with a screeching Oscar cradled in his arms. He was trying to feed the tyke a bottle of milk. The baby was having no part of it.

"Maybe a bedtime story would help," Louis muttered. "You want a bedtime story, baby?"

The baby belched.

Louis took that as a definite yes.

"Okay," he began. "Once there were these seven dwarfs and they had a limited partnership in a small mining operation, and one day this beautiful princess came to stay with them and they bartered room and board in exchange for housekeeping services, which was a very good deal for all of them because back then they didn't have to withhold tax and Social Security, and I guess she didn't have to file state and federal income-tax returns, either, which I'm not saying is *right,* you understand, because they could've got in a lot of trouble doing that, but it's just a story, so I guess it's okay."

Louis gazed down at Oscar.

The little boy had nodded out.

Louis heaved a sigh. "I can finish this later if you're tired," he advised the child.

Janine munched popcorn before the TV.

On the screen a blurb for the evening news appeared. A man with a toupee that looked like a muskrat faced the camera. "Ghosts. Are they worse than street gangs? Film and Ouija board at eleven."

22

Deep within the bowels of New York City, Stantz, Spengler, and Winston stood on an ancient train platform, their powerful flashlights blazing. They quickly unhooked themselves from the cables that had lowered them down to the ooze-laden substrata of Van Horne Station, and gazed down into the churning, glowing, whirling river of slime beneath them.

It was an awesome sight. The slime belched and bubbled, swished and swirled.

Stantz stared grimly into the "live" river. "Let's get a sounding on the depth of that flow."

Stantz grabbed a long coiled cord with a bobbing flotation device on the end. It was attached firmly to his utility belt. "Stand back," he ordered his companions.

He took the cord in his hand and, swinging the flotation device over his head, cast the line into the water like a master fisherman. The bob at the end of the line sank beneath the depths of the slime.

Spengler watched the line sink farther and farther

down, calculating the depths on a small hand-held de-vice. "Six feet. Seven feet. *Eight* feet."

The line stopped moving.

"That's it," Stantz announced. "It's on the bottom."

Suddenly the line began to wriggle again. Spengler continued to calculate. "Nine feet. Ten feet."

Winston was confused. "Is the line *still* sinking?"

Spengler gaped at the river. "No! The slime is rising."

Stantz glanced down and saw the slime climbing up over the edge of the train station platform and oozing around his boots.

"Let's get out of here, boys!" he yelled.

He made an attempt to pull the cord out of the water. The cord seemed stuck. Worse yet, the line seemed to be tugging back!

"Help me!" Stantz yelled. "It's stuck!"

Winston leapt in front of his good friend Ray and began to pull the cord as well. Winston and Stantz couldn't budge the cord from the river of slime, and slowly the slime began to pull the two men toward the edge of the platform . . . closer and closer to the bubbling, churning, *living* depths below.

Spengler tossed down his monitoring device and joined the tug of war. The three men grunted, sweated, and strained, but whatever was pulling on the cord from below was clearly stronger . . . in a superhuman way.

Stantz worked a free hand furiously, trying to cut the cord from his utility belt.

If he didn't sever the tie, he was a dead man. Or at least a very slimed man.

The cord held fast to his belt.

Stantz grimaced and attacked his belt buckle.

Quickly, frantically, he worked at the belt. Finally he yanked the entire belt from his waist.

The belt and cord were yanked toward the river of slime.

Spengler and Stantz broke free from the cord in time. Winston, however, unaware of Stantz's lifesaving move, held fast to the cord.

The startled Ghostbuster found himself yanked off his feet and high into the air.

Still clutching the cord, Winston was pulled deep down into the slime river.

"Ray!" he yelled, gurgling. "Egon!"

Stantz and Spengler glanced at each other.

"Bummer," Spengler muttered.

The two remaining Ghostbusters, summoning up every ounce of courage, dove headfirst into the swirling slime after their comrade.

Stantz and Spengler were unable to swim through the percolating muck. As helpless as flies trapped in molasses, they floated out of the station and into a swirling tide of ooze.

The slime twisted and turned, Stantz and Spengler bobbing like corks in its wake. They tried their best to surface every so often to fill their lungs with air.

Stantz squinted into the swirling stream of slime. Bobbing before him was the flailing form of Winston.

Stantz and Spengler felt the pull on their bodies lessen. The flow of ooze was slowing down. Breaking up to the surface of the slime swirl, they found themselves in a massive chamber. The end of the old New York Pneumatic Railroad line. The slime seemed to calm down, grow dormant.

Sputtering, coughing, and gagging, the three Ghostbusters floated atop the gunk at the edge of the last platform of the long-deserted transportation line.

Winston pulled himself out of the slime first. Lying on his stomach, he reached down and yanked out Stantz.

The two of them then dangled over the platform and ensnared Spengler, dragging him up out of the ocean of ooze in one violent motion.

The three lay sprawled on the platform, gagging.

"Let's retreat," Stantz whispered.

"Retreat?" Spengler coughed. "I don't know the meaning of the word. . . ."

"It means," Winston clarified, "let's get the hell out of here."

Spengler pondered this. "Oh. Okay."

Moments later the three slime-encased Ghostbusters eased their way up through a dislodged manhole cover in the center of the Upper East Side of Manhattan.

For a moment the three men sat, exhausted. The slime covering their rubber suits began to percolate.

Winston suddenly leapt to his feet, thoroughly angry. "Nice going, Ray!" he roared. "What were you trying to do, drown me?"

Stantz's body tensed. He scrambled up to face Winston. "Look, Zeddemore," he replied menacingly, "it wasn't my fault that you were too stupid to drop that line!"

Winston's blood bubbled. He shoved Ray away from him. "You better watch your mouth, man, or I'll put your lights out . . . maybe for good."

Stantz's face formed an evil sneer. "Oh, yeah? Anytime, man, anytime. Just go ahead and try it."

Egon Spengler snarled and jumped between the two of them. He raised his fists in a classic boxer's pose. "If you two are looking for a fight, you got one! Who wants to try it first? Come on, Ray. Try me, sucker."

Stantz wheeled on Spengler. "Butt out, you pencil-necked geek. I've had it with you."

Ignoring the still frothing Spengler, Stantz and Winston grabbed each other by the shoulders and began to wrestle and tussle, their movements resembling a slam-dance polka.

Spengler shook his head clear.

He knew what was happening.

Dashing between the two adversaries, he pulled them apart. "Break it up!" he commanded. "Break it up!"

His voice was so authoritative, the two fighters backed off, blinking. They were confused, addled.

"Strip!" Spengler yelled. "Right now! Get out of these clothes."

Spengler began yanking off his slicker and wading boots. Bewildered, Stantz and Winston also started to disrobe in the middle of Manhattan. Spengler stripped himself to his long johns first. When he was done, he helped the other two Ghostbusters wriggle free of their slime-encased outfits.

Spengler gathered up the discarded clothes and tossed them down the open manhole cover.

The three men, now clad only in their long under-wear, stood in the middle of the street.

They found that they weren't angry anymore.

They weren't hateful, only bewildered.

Well, also cold.

Winston rubbed his head. "What were we doing?"

He faced Stantz. "Ray, I was ready to kill you!"

Stantz's face reflected his state of mind. He was totally animated. "Don't you see? It's the *slime*. That stuff is like pure, concentrated *evil*!"

Stantz cased the street and discovered that the three Ghostbusters were standing directly in front of the Manhattan Museum of Art.

Spengler caught Stantz's eye. "And the slime," he intoned, "is all flowing right to this spot."

"What are we going to do?" Winston asked.

"We have to get Venkman involved," Stantz stated. "And *now*!"

They began to trot at a hectic pace through Central Park and toward the Upper West Side.

Twenty minutes later, at Armand's Restaurant, the maître d' felt his heart skip a beat. He was too young for a heart attack, he assured himself.

Three sweating men in long johns skidded to a halt before him. He tried to act suave. "May I help you?"

Stantz glanced into the dining room and spotted Venkman. "No," he told the maître d'. "It's all right. I see him."

The three Ghostbusters, ignoring their attire, jogged past the startled maître d' and into the restaurant.

Venkman was in the midst of pouring another toast of champagne for the now decidedly tipsy Dana when he noticed Ray, Egon, and Winston jogging forward. He shook his head from side to side. He never realized that champagne could pack that powerful a wallop.

"You should have been there, Venkman," Stantz shouted, reaching the table. "Absolutely incredible!"

Venkman snapped to. "Yeah, sorry I missed it."

He gazed at his friends in their skivvies. "I guess you guys don't know about the dress code here. It's really kind of a coat-and-tie place."

Stantz didn't hear him. "It's all over the city, Pete . . . well, actually, it'a all *under* the city."

Dana stared at the trio, her jaw agape.

"There's *rivers* of the stuff down there!" Winston yelled.

"And it's all flowing toward the museum," Spengler noted.

Spengler made a sudden move, pointing in the direction of the museum. A big glob of slime, still affixed to his hand, flew across the restaurant. It smacked a well-dressed diner directly on the schnozz.

"Sorry!" Spengler called out.

Dana came to. "Maybe we should discuss this somewhere else?"

Venkman noted the look of embarrassment on Dana's face and got up from the table. He pulled his colleagues to the side of the restaurant and whispered, "Boys, listen. You're scaring the straight crowd here. Let's save this until tomorrow, okay?"

Spengler furrowed his bushy eyebrows. "This won't wait until tomorrow, Venkman. It's hot and it's ready to pop."

Venkman glanced over Spengler's shoulder. The maître d' was leading two New York cops toward the Ghostbusters. Venkman rolled his eyes. One hell of a date.

"Arrest these men!" the maître d' commanded.

One of the cops recognized Spengler, Stantz, Winston, and Venkman. "Hey! *It's the Ghostbusters!*"

He gazed at the three men in their underwear. "Umm, but you're out of uniform, gentlemen."

Stantz, for the first time, gazed down at what he was wearing. What a disgrace! "Uh, well, we had a little accident and we . . . *but forget that!* We have to see the mayor as quickly as possible!"

The first cop withered under Stantz's determined stare. "Oh, gee, Doc. They got a big official dinner going on up there at Gracie Mansion. Maybe you should go home, get a good night's sleep, and then give the mayor a call in the morning. Whaddaya say?"

Spengler glared at the two policemen, using his "more concerned" look. "Look, we're not drunk and we're not crazy. We were almost *killed* tonight. This is a matter of vital importance!"

The two cops exchanged puzzled glances. Venkman heaved a colossal sigh. So much for romantic evenings. He marched toward the law officers, the very portrait of perfect authority. "Maybe I can straighten this out, Officers."

The two cops sighed. "Peter Venkman!" the second cop cried. "*World of the Psychic*! That's one of my two favorite shows!"

Venkman nodded. "Please! Don't tell me the other one. Just do me a favor? Get on the phone, call the mayor. Tell him the city's in danger and that if he won't see us right now, we're going to *The New York Times.*"

The first cop gasped. "What's up?"

Venkman leaned forward and collared the cop. Glancing to his left and to his right, he whispered confidentially into the policeman's ear. "Bad caviar. Tons of it. Iranian terrorists. One in every five eggs is poisoned, and we know which ones. We've got to get there before they serve the canapés."

The policeman shot Venkman a skeptical look.

Venkman didn't back down.

"Just call the mayor!"

III

*"There is no great genius
without a mixture of
madness."*

—ARISTOTLE

●

"My mind is a total void."

—WINSTON ZEDDEMORE

23

Carl Schurz Park, on the Upper East Side of Manhattan, glistened under a sparkling winter sky. The twinkling of the stars was rivaled by the flashing, blinking lights of a police cruiser as it made its way through the park on the East River at Eighty-eighth Street, the Ecto1A in close pursuit.

The two vehicles screamed into an underground parking garage leading to the mayor of New York's residence, Gracie Mansion.

The two cars sputtered to a stop in the parking area. Peter Venkman, still feeling like Douglas Fairbanks, emerged, well dressed if overly cologned, from the vehicle. His three long-johnned companions, now wearing police raincoats, were ushered into the house by a startled butler.

They were led up several flights of twisting stairs and down a hallway to a massive set of double oak doors. The butler knocked lightly and then opened the door.

Inside the antique-littered den, in front of a roaring

fireplace, sat the mayor of New York. Well coiffed, well dressed, Jack Hardemeyer stood at his side, a Doberman in *GQ* mode. Both men were wearing tuxedos, although Hardemeyer's was clearly more expensive than the mayor's.

The Ghostbusters strode into the room.

The mayor was clearly fighting back an outburst of sudden, albeit sincere, anger. He wasn't happy about being dragged out of a formal reception. He was even less happy about seeing the smirking face of Peter Venkman again.

His doctor had warned him about his blood pressure.

Right now he felt about as stable as a Pop-Tart in a microwave.

"All right," the mayor hissed. "*Ghossssstbusters.* I'll tell you right now . . . I've got two hundred of the heaviest campaign contributors in the city out there eating bad roast chicken just waiting for me to give the speech of my life. You've got two minutes. You'd better make it *good.*"

Stantz clumped forward. "Mr. Mayor, there is a psychomagnetheric slime flow of immense proportions building up under this city!"

The mayor gaped at Stantz. "Psycho *what?*"

Spengler waddled toward the mayor. "We believe that negative human emotions are materializing in the form of a viscous, semiliquid living psycho-reactive plasm with explosive supranormal potential."

The mayor heaved a heavy sigh. "Doesn't anyone speak *English* anymore?"

Winston braced himself and walked up to the mayor. "Yeah, man. What we're trying to tell you is that all the bad feelings, all the hate and anger and violence of this city, are turning into this *strange* sludge. I didn't believe it at first, either, but we just took a bath in it and we ended up almost *killing* each other."

Hardemeyer clenched his carefully shaved jaw and leapt forward. "This is *insane*," he intoned in a voice used only by Ivy League grads.

He turned to the mayor. "Do we *really* have to listen to this?"

Venkman marched into the fray. "Hey, hairball, butt out!" he said.

He stood before the mayor. "Look, Lenny, you have to admit there's no shortage of bad vibes in this town. There must be at least a couple of million miserable assholes in the tristate area."

He pointed to Hardemeyer. "And here's a good example."

Stantz joined in. "You get enough negative energy flowing in a dense environment like Manhattan and it starts to build up. If we don't do something fast, this whole place will blow up like a frog on a hot plate!"

Winston nodded. "Tell him about the toaster."

Venkman shrugged. "I don't think Lenny is ready for the toaster."

The mayor shook his head from side to side. "Being miserable and treating other people like dirt is every New Yorker's *God-given right*. I'm sorry, none of this makes any sense to me. If anything *does* happen, we've got plenty of paid professionals to deal with it. Your two minutes are up. Good night, gentlemen."

The mayor leapt out of his chair and rushed out of his den. The Ghostbusters stared at Hardemeyer. Hardemeyer ran a comb through his neatly groomed hair, offering the quartet a well-rehearsed smirk. "That's quite a story."

Venkman retorted, "Yeah, I think *The New York Times* would be interested, don't you? I know, sure as heck, that the *New York Post* would have a lot of fun with it."

Hardemeyer's eyes flipped to their "cold and calculating" stare. "Before you go running to the newspapers with your story, would you consider telling this slime epic to some people *downtown*?"

Venkman smiled. "*Now* you're talking."

Hardemeyer allowed the Ghostbusters to leave Gracie Mansion. He picked up the phone, grinning.

"I hope you geeks like straitjackets," he said with a sneer.

God, politics was a *great* life.

24

Parkview Hospital was a great place if you happened to be one card short of a full deck. Most patients either talked to themselves, took orders from extraterrestrial beings, or were sure that they were the second coming of the deity of their choice.

Since Venkman, Stantz, Spengler, and Winston didn't claim *any* of those things, they weren't too excited about being locked up in a padded cell. The four stood handcuffed in the rubber room, their cuffs firmly attached to the thick leather belts strapped tightly around their waists.

The psychiatrist in the room, a squinty-eyed man who looked like he ate flies for a living, tried to pry the truth out of Stantz, Spengler, and Winston. Venkman, having posed as a shrink once or twice in the past, knew what they were up against. He passed his time by slamming his forehead into one of the padded walls.

Stantz tried to be truthful with the psychiatrist. "We think the spirit of Vigo the Carpathian is alive in a painting at the Manhattan Museum of Art."

"I see." The psychiatrist nodded. "And are there any other paintings in the museum with bad spirits in them?"

Spengler was losing his patience with the squinty-eyed mole man. "You're wasting valuable time!" he declared. "We have reason to believe that Vigo is drawing strength from a psychomagnetheric slime flow that's been collecting under the city!"

The shrink smiled. "Yes, tell me about the slime."

"It's potent stuff," Winston said. "We made a toaster dance with it, then a bathtub tried to eat Peter's friend's baby!"

Winston pointed at Venkman. The shrink glanced in Venkman's direction. Peter stopped pounding his head for a moment. "Don't look at me. *I* think they're nuts."

The psychiatrist got up and left the cell in silence.

The four Ghostbusters stood forlornly in their cell. They had blown it and blown it in a big way. There was nothing, no one, who could save them, now.

As dawn approached, Dana Barrett tossed in her sleep at Venkman's place. Louis and Janine had remained at the apartment, not wanting to leave Dana alone and unguarded. She had spent half the night worrying about Venkman and the boys. Within the last five hours it seemed as if they had disappeared off the face of the earth.

It would be morning soon. It wasn't like Venkman not to call, especially when the stakes were so high.

Huddled in front of the TV, Louis and Janine watched a rerun of *Family Feud.*

Dana's work area in the museum stood deserted. Across the restoration studio, an impatient Janosz Poha stood before the mighty painting of Vigo. Vigo's eyes shimmered, and the portrait gradually came to life.

As usual, the first thing the thundering voice of Vigo did was to recite the litany of his power. Janosz sighed. He'd heard this all before, many times. Frankly it was beginning to appeal to him as much as a broken record.

"I, Vigo, the scourge of Carpathia, the sorrow of Moldavia, command you. . . ."

Janosz nodded. Yeah, yeah, yeah. "Command me, Lord."

"On a mountain of skulls in a castle of pain, I sat upon a throne of blood . . ."

Janosz rolled his eyes. "The skulls again."

"Twenty thousand corpses swung from my walls and parapets, and the rivers ran with tears."

The wiry artist nodded. ". . . the parapets. Yes, I know."

"By the power of the Book of Gombots, what was will be, what is will be no more. Then, now and always, the kingdom of the damned."

Janosz checked his wristwatch. "I await the word of Vigo," he muttered.

Vigo's glowing mouth began to twitch. "I have watched the centuries wither before me and waited for the time when the tide of men's sins would swell to bring me forth again. *Now* is that time and *here* the place. Beneath this realm there flows a foaming, unholy pile *born* from the *evil* in men."

Janosz's attention perked up. *This* was new.

"Upon this unholy matter," Vigo continued, "will I float the vessel of my freedom. The season of evil begins with the birth of the New Year. Bring me the child that I might live again."

Janosz found himself transfixed with awe. "Lord Vigo, this woman, Dana, is fine and strong. I was wondering—well, would it be possible?—could I have her?"

Vigo emitted a thunderous laugh. "So be it!" the spirit vowed. "On this day of darkness she will be ours! *Wife* to you. *Mother* to me!"

Vigo's laughter echoed through the restoration studio. It grew stronger and stronger, more and more Olympian.

So strong, in fact, that it reached forward into the heavens and split the sky.

Janosz looked up through the room's skylight as a strange and terrifying sight unfolded over New York.

Darkness caressed the city as the sun above it was sent, magically, into an eclipse.

At the Parkview psychiatric ward dayroom, Peter Venkman sat among a small gaggle of patients who had trouble breathing and blinking at the same time. He carefully worked at his occupational therapy, weaving on a hand loom.

Suddenly the room was plunged into darkness. Venkman wasn't pleased. "Hit the light there, Winston. I'm trying to finish my pot holder before lunch."

Winston didn't respond. He, Spengler, and Stantz stood in the center of the room, gazing through the mesh-covered windows into the newly darkened sky.

Stantz's mouth dropped open. "Total, spontaneous solar eclipse!" He gasped.

He faced his two companions. "This is it, boys. It's starting. Shit storm two thousand."

The three men faced each other, not knowing whether to feel relieved or terrified. On the down side, it was the end of the world as they knew it.

On the plus side, they'd be a lot safer in Parkview right now than anyplace on the streets of Manhattan.

25

While meteorologists, astronomers, and city officials tried to explain to a startled public exactly *why* New York had been embraced by the shadows caused by a total eclipse, the effect of Vigo's power began to make itself felt.

At a Hudson River pier, a leaky drainpipe suddenly began dripping shimmering, pulsating slime into the river near the Cunard Line docks.

Shortly thereafter, at the refurbished Central Park Zoo, the polar bears, lounging in their outdoor cage, lazily allowed a zookeeper to hose down their mountainous terrain. The zookeeper put down the hose and started to sweep around the top of their cage. Unbeknownst to him, the water the hose was gushing grew thicker and stranger, sparkling and undulating. Slime. Lots of it.

By the time the zookeeper finished sweeping the upper reaches of the outside enclosure, he was vaguely aware that something was wrong. He turned to pick up his hose. There was no water running out of it.

It was bone-dry.

He heard a screech coming from nearby.

He spun around and jumped back in surprise.

A full-sized pterodactyl screamed at him and then launched itself up into the dark, cloud-laden sky.

The zookeeper made a beeline for the exit door.

The polar bears exchanged startled glances. New York sure wasn't like the Arctic!

At Fifty-ninth and Fifth, the massive fountain located across from the swank Plaza Hotel suddenly began to change color. Instead of water zooming up out of its spout, torrents of psycho-reactive slime emerged, splashing, cascading, and oozing all over the surrounding sidewalk.

At the Plaza Hotel, a well-heeled man and woman emerged from a limousine. As they walked up the front steps leading to the hotel, a wad of slime landed on the woman's luxurious full-length mink coat.

As the doorman eased the front door open with a bow, the woman yelped in pain.

"Something *bit* me!" she said, glaring at the startled doorman.

The doorman looked curiously at her. He yelled in terror and leapt backward as the woman's slimed coat quivered to life. Small, ferocious mink heads popped out of the thick fur, snarling, barking, and yapping. Their sharp little teeth nipped at the air.

Reacting quickly, the doorman yanked the coat off the woman's back and threw it onto the sidewalk. He tried to stomp the coat to death, but the beady-eyed varmints in the coat were too quick for him.

As the doorman, the woman, and her husband looked on, flummoxed, the mink coat, its hydra-head of critters snapping and snarling, skittered off, trotting down Fifth Avenue with a vengeance.

The woman glared at her husband. "I told you we should have stayed in Palm Beach," she said, her face ashen.

At the Midtown North Police Precinct, a squad room filled with busy detectives noticed a change in the flood of calls they were receiving.

Initially they were trying to explain just what a total eclipse *was* and *wasn't.*

For the past hour, however, the calls had gotten a tad more, er, squirrelly.

"Look, lady," said one cop into the phone. "Of course there are dead people there. It's a cemetery. . . . What? . . . They were asking you for *directions*?"

"Was this a big dinosaur or a little dinosaur?" another cop asked. "Oh, just a skeleton, huh? Heading toward Central Park?"

Another detective sighed and shook his head. "Wait a second. You say the park bench was chasing you? You mean someone was chasing you in the park, don't you? . . . No, the bench itself was galloping after you. I see. . . ."

He raised his eyes to heaven and pushed the hold button on his phone. He called to his lieutenant, "Sir? I think you better talk to this guy."

The lieutenant faced the cop. "I have problems of my own."

"What's up?"

"It's some dock supervisor down at Pier 34 on the Hudson. The guy's going nuts!"

"What's the problem?"

"He says the *Titanic* just arrived!"

"Car 54 is in the area, isn't it, Lieutenant? Can't you just have him check it out?"

"Good idea."

Moments later two uniformed patrolmen and a very

stunned dock supervisor stared out at the Hudson River. There, moored to a dock, was an ocean liner bearing the name R.M.S. *Titanic.* The gangplank was lowered and hundreds of long-drowned passengers disembarked. They were sopping wet and drenched with seaweed. Behind them, cadaverous porters off-loaded water-logged baggage.

"I don't believe this," one cop said to another.

"And look at the water," the dock supervisor said. "It almost looks solid. It's spooky, Officers. Damned spooky!"

"Who're we gonna call?" the second replied.

"The lieutenant!" the first cop declared.

He ran to his squad car and began dialing the precinct. Beyond him, all hell was breaking loose in New York City.

. . . and that was just for starters.

26

Dana sat, curled in the couch before Venkman's battered TV set, watching a *Star Trek* rerun. Janine and Louis continued to munch popcorn. Every so often the network would interrupt with a local bulletin announcing that nobody in New York—or America, for that matter—knew what the heck was going on in the streets outside Dana's window.

"Mass hysteria" was how one wild-eyed reporter phrased it.

Dana grew uneasy as she watched the television. She should have heard from Venkman by now. The sky outside the window was dark and foreboding.

Without warning, a howling gust of wind blew open the French windows in Venkman's living room.

"What the. . . ?" Louis yelped.

Dana heard the baby cry out. A sense of alarm welled up within her. Oscar!

She hurried to the bedroom to check on her son, a frantic Louis and Janine trailing behind her.

The bed was empty.

Oscar was nowhere in sight.

The windows to the bedroom, however, were open.

Dana, Louis, and Janine ran to the window and peered outside.

"Oh, my God," Janine said, pointing.

Dana glanced to her left. On the ledge, towering above the busy streets of lower Manhattan, crawled little Oscar.

He knelt on the very edge of the ledge at the corner of the building, some fifty feet above the ground. The baby seemed calm, almost expectant.

Dana took a deep breath and climbed out onto the ledge, bracing her back against the strong support of the building. She daren't look down. She was afraid of losing her nerve. Slowly, cautiously, she inched her way along the eight-inch-wide ledge.

A bubbling light flared up in the sky above her, causing her to stop in her tracks.

An apparition was forming.

Something straight out of a fairy tale.

A sweet, kindly-looking English nanny formed in the sky, pushing an old-fashioned, albeit transparent baby carriage. The woman was strolling on thin air toward the ledge, dozens of feet above any solid matter.

The woman was smiling.

Dana gaped, recognizing the smile and trying to place the face.

The airborne nanny marched through the sky directly toward little Oscar. She extended a strong hand and deftly snatched up Dana's baby.

The nanny drew a delighted little Oscar into the transparent carriage, turning and smiling at a startled Dana.

"No!" Dana screamed.

She watched in helpless horror as the nanny soared

off into the darkened skies, little Oscar huddled securely in the ethereal baby buggy.

The nanny chuckled.

Dana snapped to. She recognized the smile. She recognized the chuckle. She recognized the face!!!

"Janosz!" she breathed.

Louis and Janine helped Dana back inside the apartment. She headed straight for the door. "Louis, you have to find Peter and tell him what happened!"

"Where are you going?"

"To get my baby back," Dana said, slamming the door behind her.

Meanwhile, seated silently around a table in Parkview's woo-woo ward dayroom, Venkman, Winston, Stantz, and Spengler carefully listened to the conversations offered by the newest members of the laughing academy.

The squinty-eyed shrink had his hands full. A well-heeled woman who claimed she was a guest at the Plaza Hotel was screaming at him.

"I'm telling you, Doctor, my mink coat bit me and ran off down the street!"

The doctor was clearly out of his league. He turned to a nearby nurse. "Where did you put the zookeeper who saw the pterodactyl?"

The nurse sighed. "He's in Room 5, and I have the three men who saw the *Titanic* in Rooms 10, 11, and 12."

She consulted her list. "The walking-dead witness is in 13, the strolling dinosaur skeleton is in 4. I seem to have misplaced the Elvis Presley spotter, though."

The doctor sighed. "I hate working on New Year's Eve. It really brings them out of the woodwork, doesn't it?"

"I think that eclipse thing has everybody spooked," the nurse replied.

"What about my coat?" the Plaza woman yelled. "Do you have any idea how much that coat cost?"

The Ghostbusters sat at the table, listening intently.

Venkman turned to Stantz. "You were right. The whole city is going nuts. If we don't do something fast, it's all going to go downhill from here."

Winston nodded. "Do you think all those predictions about the world coming to an end in the 1990s are true?"

A Parkview patient with a face resembling a jack-o-lantern waddled up to them. "The year will be 1997. My *dog* told me."

"What kind of dog?" Venkman asked.

"Labrador."

Venkman shook his head sadly. "Habitual liars. They can't help it. It's in the breed."

The man nodded sadly and stumbled off. Spengler faced his colleagues. "Objectively speaking, all these apocalyptic predictions about the millennium make no sense at all. The year 2000 is a fiction based on a completely arbitrary calendar. The only thing that gives these predictions power is people's willingness to believe in them!"

Stantz agreed. "Sure. If everyone believes that things are going to start falling apart in the year 2000, they'll probably start falling apart."

Winston rubbed his chin. "Yeah, well, there are an awful lot of people out there who *don't* believe in the future anymore—their own or anybody else's."

"And that's where Vigo gets his power," Stantz deduced. "He's just been laying back, hiding in that jerky painting until enough bad vibes built up to spring him."

"I don't think there's any shortage of bad vibes in *this* town," Venkman replied. "This is one of the few towns where killing your landlord is considered a misdemeanor."

Spengler stared at his knuckles thoughtfully. "All Vigo needs now is a living human being to inhabit. He's had his eye on Dana, literally. So it's obvious that he's chosen Dana's child to make his reentry into our world. We all know that she has a psychic vulnerability to hostile entities. She's probably passed that onto her baby. Janosz Poha may be the human link between Vigo and Dana."

Venkman sneered. "I *knew* that guy was a wiggler the second I laid my eyes on him."

A thin Parkview patient leaned over the Ghostbusters' table. "Forget Vigo," he whispered confidentially. "It's *Hitler* you should go after. I saw him hanging around the Port Authority."

"Where was he heading?" Venkman asked.

"New Jersey," the man said. "I think it was the 134 local bus."

"Thanks for the info," Venkman said, offering a crooked smile.

Downstairs in a Parkview examining room, Louis Tully was arguing with his cousin Sherman, a badly dressed and coiffed gnat of a man who defined the word "nebbish" almost as well as Louis did.

"Come on, Sherm," Louis whined. "You're my cousin. Do this for me. I'm begging you."

Sherman shook his head, flashing a superior smile. "I can't do it, Louis. It isn't ethical. I could lose my license."

"Why can't you just have them released? You're a doctor."

"I'm a dermatologist. I can't write orders for the psych ward."

"Sherman, I've done lots of favors for you, haven't I?" Louis wheedled.

"Like what?"

"I got you out of those bad tax shelters."

"*You* were the one who got me in."

"I fixed you up with Diane Troxler, and she put out, didn't she?"

Sherman thought hard about this. "Yeah, I had to give her free dermabrasion for a year too. Forget it, Louis. I could get in a lot of trouble."

"I'm telling you, Sherm, we're all going to be in big trouble if we don't do something fast. This ghost guy came and took my friend's baby and we've got to get it back. It's just a scared little baby, Sherm."

"Then you should go to the police," Sherman pointed out. "I don't believe in any of that ghost stuff."

Outside the window, shrieks and howls echoed through the darkened sky. The city seemed to grow darker and darker and darker.

Sherman faced the window. He could have sworn he saw a pterodactyl fly by.

"Do you believe now, Sherm?"

A half hour later the four Ghostbusters, in full uniform, stood next to Ecto1A, together with the Tully cousins. "Good work, Louis. How did you get us out?"

"Oh, I pulled a few strings. I wouldn't want to say more than that."

Louis winked at Sherman. "This is my cousin Sherman. Sherm, say hello to the Ghostbusters."

Louis leaned toward Stantz. "I promised him a ride in the car if he got you out."

"How bad are things getting?" Venkman asked.

"Real bad, Peter. You'd better get to the museum right away!"

"Why? What happened?" Venkman asked.

"A ghost took Dana's baby. She's gone to the museum to get it back."

Louis pointed to the Ecto1A. "I brought everything you asked for, and I gassed up the car with super unleaded. It cost twenty cents more than regular unleaded, but you get much better performance and in an old car like this, that'll end up saving you money in the long run. I put it on my credit card, so you can either reimburse me or I can take it out of petty cash."

The four stone-faced Ghostbusters, fully suited and well armed, dove into the Ecto1A and sped off, leaving Louis in mid-sentence.

Louis watched the car speed away. "Hey!" he shouted. "Wait for me."

The auto zoomed out of sight.

Louis sighed. "Okay, I'll meet you there."

Sherman stared at his cousin skeptically. "I thought you were like the fifth Ghostbuster."

Louis smiled smugly. "I let them handle all the little stuff. I just come in on the big cases."

27

Dana Barrett jumped out of her cab and rushed up the front stairs to the Manhattan Museum of Art. She flung open two large doors and dashed inside. The doors closed behind her with a resounding *ka-thud*. As the doors locked themselves shut, a deafening roar of thunder shook the sky. The ground seemed to tremble.

From deep within the earth beneath the museum, small, slender hands of glowing, shimmering slime reached up toward the building's walls.

The slime burst forth from the bowels of the city and crept and crawled up and over the building.

Within seconds the slime had completely engulfed the museum, effectively sealing Dana inside.

Two passersby stopped before the museum, a pair of old men out for an early-evening stroll.

"Now that's something you don't see every day, Mike," one said to the other.

"What's that, Al?"

"An ocean of goop scooping up and over a museum."

"Hmm." The second man nodded. "And it seems to be hardening too."

"Think we should call the cops?"

"I dunno. What time is *Moonlighting* on?"

"We got time. Come on, there's a phone booth over there. I used to walk my poodle there, until she got mugged by squirrels."

"I hate rodents."

"Me too. I never even liked Mickey Mouse."

"Me neither. Although I always liked Mighty Mouse. He has a great voice."

The two old men strolled to the phone booth.

By the time the Ecto1A screeched up to the curb across from the beleaguered museum, hundreds of spectators had gathered. They stood in awe, gawking at the slime-encased building. The four Ghostbusters leapt out of their vehicle and jogged across the street.

They stood spellbound at the sight before them.

The museum was now totally covered in a shell of psycho-reactive slime. City workmen and firemen were trying to cut their way through the hardened gunk with a series of blowtorches, jackhammers, and assorted power tools. Paramedics were on the scene, attempting to munch through the solid slime using the "jaws of life."

They couldn't even make a dent.

The Ghostbusters retreated to the Ecto1A and donned their proton packs.

"It looks like a giant Jell-O mold," Stantz breathed.

"I hate Jell-O," Venkman replied.

"I'm not even crazy about Bill Cosby," Winston said, grimacing.

The quartet strode across the street and approached the main entrance to the building.

Stantz walked up to a bewildered fire captain. "Okay, give it a rest, sir. We'll take it from here."

The fire captain was clearly skeptical. "Be my guest, gents," he said with a smirk. "We've been cutting here for almost an hour. What the hell is going on around this town? Did you know that the *Titanic* arrived this morning?"

Venkman shrugged. "Better late than never."

The workmen and firemen assembled before the slime-encrusted museum backed away as the Ghostbusters aimed their powerful particle throwers.

Spengler whipped out his Giga meter. He nodded grimly to his three comrades. "Full neutronas, maser assist!"

The four men adjusted the settings on their wands and prepared to fire.

Stantz gritted his teeth. "Throw 'em!"

The four men triggered their particle throwers and sprayed the front doors of the building with powerful, undulating bolts of proton energy. The energy beams bounced harmlessly off the hardened slime.

Venkman sighed and turned to a fireman. "Okay, who knows 'Kumbaya'?"

A few of the firemen and workmen tentatively raised their hands. Venkman grabbed them and lined them up at the entrance to the museum, assuming a drill sergeant's voice. "All right, men. Nice and easy. 'Kumbaya, my Lord, Kumbaya . . .'"

Stantz, Spengler, Winston, and the firemen and workmen began to sing along.

Venkman forced them all to join hands and to sway back and forth while lifting their voices to the night sky.

Stantz ran forward during the folkfest and inspected

the hardened wall of slime that entombed the museum. Using his infra-goggles, he found that the singing had managed to produce a hole in the gunk barely the size of a dime.

Stantz sighed and turned to the assembled. "Forget it. The Vienna Boys Choir couldn't get through this stuff."

"Good effort," Venkman called to the hastily assembled ensemble. He turned to his buddies. "Now what? Should we say supportive, nurturing things to it, Ray?"

Spengler, deep in thought, missed the sarcasm. "It won't work," he muttered. "There's no way we could generate enough positive energy to crack that shell."

Stantz wasn't convinced. Ever the optimist, he cried, "I can't believe things have gotten *so* bad in this city that there's no way back. Sure, it's crowded, it's dirty, it's noisy. And there are too many people who'd just as soon step on your face as look at you. But there's got to be a few sparks of sweet humanity left in this burned-out burg. We just have to *mobilize* them!"

Spengler nodded in agreement. "We need something that everyone can get behind. You know, a *symbol* . . ."

Spengler's eyes accidentally fell on Ecto1A's New York State license plates. On the front plate was a line drawing of the historic Statue of Liberty.

He nudged Stantz. Stantz gaped at the plate. "Something that appeals to the best in each and every one of us," he babbled.

"Something good," Spengler continued.

"And pure," Venkman added.

"And decent," Winston concluded.

The four men were awakened from their reverie by a murmur in the vast crowd behind them. A limo screamed up to the site. The mayor of New York arrived with a police escort. His limo pulled into a no-parking zone. The mayor and Jack Hardemeyer stepped out of the limo and marched up to the museum entrance.

Hardemeyer motioned the mayor back.

The top aide, with a small army of police body-guards, ambled up to the Ghostbusters, confrontation clearly the goal.

"Look," the well-tailored Hardemeyer spat, "I've had it with you *Ghostbusters*. Get your stuff together, get back in your clown car, and get out of here. This is a city matter, and everything's under control."

Venkman felt his blood start to boil. He stared down the yuppie-pup. "Oh," he said with a sneer, "you *think* so? Well, I've got news for you. You've got Dracula's brother-in-law in there, and he's got my girlfriend and her kid. Around about midnight tonight, while you guys are partying hearty uptown, *this* guy's going to come to life and start doing amateur head transplants. And *that*'s just round one."

The mayor traipsed forward. "Are you telling me there are people *trapped* in that building?"

Hardemeyer ignored the mayor. He turned to one of his flunkies. "This is dynamite," he said enthusiastically. "I want you to call AP, UPI, and the CNN network. I want them down here right away. When the police bring this kid and his mama out, I want to be able to hand the baby right over to the mayor, and I want it all on camera."

Stantz wasn't impressed with Hardemeyer's approach. He turned to the mayor. "Mr. Mayor, if we don't do something by midnight tonight, you're going to go down in history as the man who let New York get sucked down into the tenth level of *hell*!"

The mayor considered this. He turned to the fire captain. "Can you get into that museum?"

The fire captain offered a sad smile. "If I had a nuclear warhead . . . *maybe.*"

The mayor turned to Venkman.

"You know why all these things are happening?"

Venkman was angry now. "We tried to tell you *last* night, but Mr. Hard-on over here had us packed off to a loony bin."

Hardemeyer felt himself losing it. He didn't care. The Ghostbusters were his enemies. "This is preposterous!" he whined. "You can't seriously believe all this mumbo jumbo, Mr. Mayor. It's the twentieth century, for crying out loud!"

He bared his teeth to Venkman. "Look, *mister,* I don't know what this stuff is or how you got it all over the museum, but you'd better get it off *now,* and I mean *right now*!"

Hardemeyer ran up to the museum's entrance like a madman possessed. He began to pound at the wall of slime with his fists.

Both the mayor and the Ghostbusters watched in amazement as the wall of slime seemed to give in for a fleeting instant. Hardemeyer's fist plunged through the wall. He flashed a defiant sneer at Venkman. His sneer, however, soon turned to something more closely resembling the letter *O.*

Within seconds the wall promptly sucked Hardemeyer inside the slime curtain, emitting a gushy, *slooooshing* sound.

Before anyone had the time to react, Hardemeyer was gone.

Only his three-hundred-dollar shoes remained . . . hanging from the re-hardened wall of slime.

The mayor of New York emitted a heavy sigh. He turned to the Ghostbusters. "Okay," he whispered, "just tell me what you need."

28

The quartet of Ghostbusters sat stone-faced in the tiny diner with the mayor of New York City.

The mayor was sweating.

The Ghostbusters regarded him coolly.

Outside the small burger joint, a dozen security men patrolled silently.

The mayor was nearly in a state of panic. "Did you know the *Titanic* arrived this morning?"

Venkman nodded. "So I've heard, and I bet all the hotels have weird bookings . . . this being New Year's Eve and all."

"Don't get cute with me." The mayor barked. "Just tell me why all these things are happening!"

Venkman sipped his coffee. "We *tried* to, Yer Honor. But you wouldn't believe us. I don't wanna get too technical here, but basically, things are going to hell because people in New York act like *jerks*."

The mayor nearly swallowed his catsup-covered weenie. "What?"

Stantz smiled sweetly at the paranoid politician.

"Imagine an ocean's worth of bad vibes being poured into a small glass, the glass being this city. That's the situation we're up against. We have about four hours before that glass, under pressure from the flow, *shatters.*"

Winston took the opportunity to thrust a mighty forefinger into the mayor's chest. "Plus, you've got one mean lean Carpathian mother in that museum who is just *ready* and *willing* to pick up the pieces and go *gung ho.*"

The mayor emitted a small moan. "And it had to happen in an election year. Well, who is this guy and what does he want?"

Stantz stared at the mayor. "He wants it *all.* In every great social breakdown there has been some evil, power-mad nutball ready to capitalize on it. This one just happens to have been dead for at least three hundred years."

"It's happened before," Spengler informed the mayor. "Nero and Caligula in Rome. Hitler in Nazi Germany . . ."

Stantz jumped in. "Stalin in Russia. The French Reign of Terror!"

Winston decided to put his two cents in: "Pol Pot? Idi Amin?"

Venkman turned toward the fidgeting mayor. "Cardinal Richelieu, George Steinbrenner, Donald Trump!"

The mayor caved in, his face resembling a three-day-old Mr. Potato Head. "But being miserable and stomping on people's dreams is every New Yorker's *right* . . . isn't it? What do you expect me to do? Go on the TV and tell eight million people that all of a sudden they have to be *nice* to each other?"

Venkman grinned, crocodile-style. "Naaaah. We'll handle that part. We only need *one* thing from you."

The mayor nodded up and down, like a Slinky toy.

He felt a sudden surge of relief. Dr. Venkman only needed *one* thing from him. Maybe the mayor would come out of this looking okay. Maybe next year's election wouldn't be affected.

Then Venkman explained what the Ghostbusters needed.

At that point the mayor fainted.

29

Behind the Ghostbusters, the skyline of Manhattan sparkled radiantly, ready to embrace the New Year. They stood at the feet of the Statue of Liberty on Liberty Island, donning their new equipment. They strapped compression tanks to their backs and hooked up nozzles from their backpacks to the bazookalike weapons Stantz and Spengler had created. They adjusted the gauges, valves, and regulators on the prototypes of the latest ghostbusting weapons.

Weapons that were untested.

Weapons they had never used before.

Slime blowers.

Venkman tightened the shoulder straps on the slime blower, gazing up at the Statue of Liberty. "Kind of makes you wonder, doesn't it?"

"Wonder what?" Winston asked.

"If she's naked under that toga," Venkman replied. "She's French, you know."

Spengler missed the humor. "There's nothing under that toga but three hundred tons of iron and steel."

Venkman's face fell. Another dream dashed.

Stantz was clearly worried about their hastily conceived plan of attack. "I hope we have enough stuff to do the job."

"Only one way to find out," Venkman said, facing Stantz. "Ready, Teddy?"

Venkman and Stantz entered the base of the statue and began the long, torturous climb up the spiraling iron staircase within Lady Liberty. The staircase corkscrewed some one hundred feet inside the hollow superstructure.

Down below, at the base of the statue, Spengler and Winston assembled hundreds of wires connected to dozens of relays. They carefully mounted the relays to the interior of the gigantic structure.

At the top of the stairs, Venkman and Stantz installed large auditorium-sized loudspeakers on a section of the statue near Lady Liberty's head.

That done, Stantz raised his slime blower and gazed at the interior of the Statue of Liberty. "Okay, boys," he commanded. "Let's frost it."

Venkman and Stantz let loose with wave after wave of psycho-reactive slime. Venkman watched the slime ooze down the interior of the statue, hoping that the plan worked.

Hoping that he and his ghostbusting buddies had the wherewithal to save Dana and her child.

Across the river, in the slime-encrusted museum, Janosz smiled in front of the massive portrait of his master, Vigo. Dana sat helplessly in a corner, watching her baby float, suspended in midair, below the horrible face of Vigo.

Janosz, brush in hand, walked merrily up to the baby and carefully began painting mystical symbols on its little arms and legs.

Dana felt faint.

The symbols were identical to the ones Janosz had uncovered on the ancient portrait.

Unable to take it any longer, she made a mad dash for her child, arms outstretched.

Before she could make it to little Oscar, she was hit full force by some sort of invisible energy. She was thrown across the room, back into her chair.

She collapsed in a heap. What had happened to the Ghostbusters? Why hadn't she heard from Louis?

Louis Tully stood proudly in the Ghostbusters' firehouse. With Janine watching adoringly, he slipped into a Ghostbusters uniform and slung a heavy proton pack onto his back, nearly knocking off his glasses. Louis tested out his mobility, waddling around the lab area on a slight angle. Janine was now worried. There was too much power pack and not enough Louis.

"I'm not sure this is such a good idea," she told him. "Do the others know that you're doing this?"

Louis nodded. "Oh, yeah, sure . . . well, *no*. But there's really not much to do here, and they might need some backup at the museum."

He adjusted his glasses, pulled up his socks, and headed for the front door.

Janine ran up to him. "You're very brave, Louis. Good luck."

Janine kissed Louis tenderly.

His glasses fogged. "Uh, well, I, uh, better hurry."

Louis dashed out of the firehouse fully armed and marched manfully into the night. . . . Where, fifteen minutes later, he caught a bus to take him to the museum.

"I'm not sure I have the right change here, but believe me this is important and—"

He sniffed the air.

Behind the steering wheel of the bus was Slimer.

Slimer sent the bus roaring down the street.

"You're going in the wrong direction!" Louis whined. "I bet you never even got a real driver's license!!"

30

Venkman, Stantz, Spengler, and Winston stood apprehensively in the observation windows of the Statue of Liberty. Perched in the crown of Lady Liberty, they gazed down at Liberty Island, far below them.

"It's now or never," Stantz whispered. He plugged in a huge cable that fed into a portable transformer. He checked his watch. "It's all yours, Pete. There's not much time left."

Venkman nodded and attached a speaker cable into his tiny tape recorder. He snapped his fingers and tapped his left foot. "Okay, a one, and a two, and a three, and a *four*!"

He pushed the play button on his Walkman, and instantly the interior of the statue was filled with the soulful strains of Jackie Wilson.

As the sweet soul music echoed through the statue's hollow interior, the slime dripping from its sides began to vibrate.

Slowly, magically, the head of the Statue of Liberty

173

turned this way and that. The Ghostbusters held on to the railing of the observation deck for dear life.

"She's moving!" Stantz exclaimed.

Winston was awestruck. "I've lived in New York all my life and I never visited the Statue of Liberty. Now I finally get here and we're taking her out for a *walk*!"

Spengler clutched his Giga meter. "We've got full power."

Stantz picked up the control paddle from a home video game and started pushing buttons. Venkman picked up a hand-held microphone. "Okay, Libby," he commanded, "let's get in *gear*."

The statue quivered in response. Lady Liberty raised a titanic left foot and brought it splashing down into the Hudson River. Her right foot followed suit.

Soon Liberty Island was deserted.

New Year's Eve celebrants on the shore of New York City, waiting for the traditional fireworks display, were astounded. The Statue of Liberty was *swimming* toward New York!

Lady Liberty walked calmly across the bottom of the Hudson, almost completely submerged. Only her head, from the nose up, was visible, the four Ghostbusters navigating her movements from the observation deck.

The water seemed to be rising rapidly toward them.

"How deep does it get?" Winston asked. "That water's cold and I can't swim."

"It's okay. I have my senior lifesaving card," Venkman said reassuringly.

Spengler couldn't help himself. He started calculating. "Let's see, with a water temperature of forty degrees, we'd survive approximately fifteen minutes."

Stantz had a maritime navigational chart spread out

before him. "I'll keep to the middle of the channel. We're okay to Fifty-ninth Street. Then we'll go ashore and crosstown and take First Avenue to Seventy-ninth."

"Are you kidding?" Venkman replied. "We'll hit all that bridge traffic at Fifty-ninth. Take Seventy-second straight across to Fifth. Trust me, I used to drive a cab."

Stantz continued to maneuver the statue. Jackie Wilson's voice boomed within Lady Liberty's hollow shell. The mood slime continued bopping.

In Times Square, thousands of people stood shoulder to shoulder, noisemakers and confetti in hand. All eyes were glued to the gigantic clock high above their heads. In ten minutes the crowd would begin the countdown for New Year's.

Suddenly one spectator pointed.

Then another, and another.

From downtown, heading north, marched the most magnificent of sights. The Statue of Liberty was walking up Broadway, striding in step to the superamplified song "Higher and Higher."

A great cheer arose from the crowd. Party hats and confetti were tossed into the air as the crowd began to dance and sing along with Jackie Wilson.

Inside the observation deck, Spengler grinned, checking his Giga meter. "Listen to that crowd! The positive GEVs are climbing."

Venkman patted the statue. "They love you, Lib. Keep it up."

The colossal statue headed up Broadway toward Central Park. From there Lady Liberty would be a hop, skip, and a jump away from the Manhattan Museum of Art.

Much to Venkman's amazement, half of the New Year's Eve celebrants from Times Square decided to follow Lady Liberty. He couldn't blame them. They probably didn't get a chance to see something like this too often.

Lady Liberty and the throngs proceeded toward the museum.

Farther uptown, the museum, still slime-encrusted, stood, guarded by police.

Inside the darkened building, Dana watched her child dangle in midair before Vigo. Janosz walked up to her, smiling. "No harm will come to the child," he assured her. "You might even say it's a privilege for him to be the vessel for the spirit of Vigo. And you . . . well, you will be the mother of the ruler of the world. Doesn't that sound nice?"

"If this is what the world will be like, I don't want to live in it," Dana vowed.

Janosz glanced over his shoulder at Vigo. "I don't believe we have the luxury of choice."

"*Everybody* has a choice," Dana said, simmering.

"Not in this case, my dear," Janosz pointed out. "Take a look at that portrait. That's not Gainsborough's *Blue Boy* up there. That's *Vigo*."

"I don't care who he is. I may not be able to stop you, but someone will!"

Janosz smirked. "Who? The Ghostbusters? They are powerless. Soon it will be midnight and the city will be mine . . . and Vigo's. Well, mainly *Vigo's* . . . but we have a spectacular opportunity to make the best of our relationship."

Dana looked the wiry artist in the eye. "We don't have a relationship."

"I know," Janosz agreed. "Marry me, Dana, and together we will raise Vigo as our son. There are many perks that come with being the mother of a living god. I'm sure he will supply for us a magnificent apartment. And perhaps a car and free parking."

Dana pushed the man away. "I hate and despise you and everything you stand for with all my heart and soul. I could never forgive what you've done to me and my child."

Janosz thought about that. "Many marriages begin with a certain amount of distance, but after a while I believe we could learn to love each other. Think about it."

"I'd rather not."

Janosz didn't mind Dana's aloofness. She'd come around once Vigo was reborn. There was nothing that could spoil Vigo's plan for conquest.

Janosz didn't notice the slight vibration in the floor beneath his feet.

The source of the vibration strode up Fifth Avenue, led by a squadron of screaming police motorcycles, with tens of thousands of cheering people marching in her wake.

Lady Liberty, still walking in step to Jackie Wilson's percussive beat.

From the observation deck the Ghostbusters could spot the museum.

"So far, so good," Venkman said.

"I'm worried," Spengler muttered. "The vibrations could shake her to pieces. We should have padded her feet."

"I don't think they make Reeboks in her size," Stantz replied.

Venkman patted the statue. "We're almost there, Lib."

He turned to Stantz. "Step on it."

Stantz diddled with his controls. Lady Liberty's foot

came crashing down on a police car. Stantz grimaced. He
called down to the startled police in the street. "My fault!"

"She's new in town," Venkman added.

He glanced at his watch. The Ghostbusters had less
than one minute left to save Dana, her child, and the
world in general.

31

The crowd at Times Square began counting down the final seconds left in the old year. Ten, nine, eight, seven . . .

In the Restoration Studio of the museum, Janosz also watched the large wall clock while painting the last of the mystical symbols on the levitated baby's chest.

Soon the world would be *his* . . . well, *partly* his.

He glanced at the portrait of Vigo. A strange aura began to spread over the painting. Vigo's eyes glowed. His entire body seemed to radiate energy. The figure in the painting began to spread its arms wide. Slowly but powerfully, Vigo's mighty torso began to assume three dimensions. Vigo was *pulling* himself out of the painting.

His long-dead lungs emitted a mighty, stagnant breath of long-rotting air. "Soon," Vigo intoned, "my life *begins*! Then, woe to the *weak*! All power to me. The world is *mine.*"

Vigo extended a bloodstained hand toward baby Oscar. The baby's body began to glow eerily as Vigo's hand approached it. Dana let out a sob. She had lost. She had lost everything that had ever mattered to her.

Janosz emitted a wheezing laugh.

He was caught in mid-wheeze as a large shadow fell over the room. He gaped up through the skylight.

The Statue of Liberty stood towering above the museum, a look of righteous anger on her freedom-loving face.

The statue knelt down next to the museum and, drawing back its titanic right arm, smashed into the ceiling with its torch of freedom.

Janosz let out a feral screech and skittered away, hiding his head from the shower of broken glass and debris. From out of the sky, the four Ghostbusters swung into the room on ropes attached to Lady Liberty's crown.

Stantz, Venkman, Spengler, and Winston trained their slime blowers on Janosz.

The wiry artist tried to retreat.

Dana leapt into action, running across the studio and diving at her child, effectively snatching floating Oscar from Vigo's outstretched, murderous hand.

Dana and her child tumbled onto the floor safely.

Venkman sneered at Janosz. "Happy New Year."

Janosz trotted in front of Vigo's animated portrait. His master would save him. Vigo bellowed in rage.

Spengler found himself grinning at both the ghoul and his human henchman. "Feel free to try something stupid."

With Vigo to back him up, Janosz now felt powerful. "You pitiful miserable creatures! You dare to challenge the power of Darkness?"

Janosz emitted a harsh cackle. "Don't you realize what you are dealing with? He's *Vigo!* You are like the buzzing of flies to him!"

Venkman shook his head sadly. "Oh, Johnny, did *you* back the wrong horse."

With that the four Ghostbusters let loose with their slime blowers, hosing down Janosz from head to toe. The force of the flying mood slime knocked Janosz across the room.

The four men then turned to the twitching, roaring portrait of Vigo. Vigo was now almost completely solid, almost free of his prison. He was now held in the portrait only from his knees down. He spat and bellowed at the Ghostbusters, trying to unleash his black-magical powers full tilt.

The Ghostbusters stood firm, secure in the knowledge that the source of Vigo's power had been neutralized by the love and goodwill of the people of New York.

"You will be destroyed!" Vigo roared.

Stantz walked forward. "Viggy, Viggy, Viggy, you have been a *bad* little monkey."

Venkman smiled at the sputtering painting. "The whole city's together on this one, Your Rottenness. We took a vote. Everybody's down on you. The people have spoken."

"So"—Winston smiled, raising his slime blower—"say good night now."

Vigo roared and, focusing his magic directly down on Stantz, transformed the stunned Ray into a sputtering, wild-eyed demon. Demon Ray leapt in front of the painting. "The power of Vigo is *greater* than anything you *wield*," demon Ray howled. *"We will destroy you!"*

"Don't shoot!" Spengler yelled. "You'll hit *Ray*!

Winston, the nearest to the portrait, inhaled and, gritting his teeth, fired the slime blower. Both Ray and Vigo were coated with a thick layer of ooze.

Vigo bellowed and howled at the sky. His body

began to quiver and shake. He felt his strength ebbing. His hands went numb. Ray Stantz was sent tumbling onto the floor. Vigo emitted one last primal howl and then fell back onto the canvas, solidly one-dimensional and harmless.

The paint on the canvas began to bubble and melt. It dribbled slowly down the portrait and onto the floor. Parts of another painting, one done years earlier on the same canvas, began to reveal itself.

Venkman, Spengler, and Winston rushed over to Ray and knelt beside him. Stantz was completely inundated with slime.

"He's breathing," Spengler said.

Winston wiped the mood slime off Ray's face. Stantz blinked and stared at his three friends.

"Ray," Winston whispered. "Ray! How do you feel?"

Stantz smiled beatifically. "Groovy. I've never felt better in my life, man."

Venkman rolled his eyes skyward. "Oh, no. We've got to *live* with *this*?"

The Ghostbusters helped Ray to his feet. Stantz beamed at them all. "I love you guys. You're the best friends I've ever had."

Stantz hugged each one of his buddies, leaving a residue of slime on them all. Venkman pushed him away. "Hey, I just had this suit cleaned!"

From across the room Janosz emitted a low moan. Venkman turned to Winston and Spengler. "Take care of the wiggler, will you?"

Venkman walked over to Dana. She cradled Oscar in her arms and gave Venkman a big hug. "What is this?" he asked. "A love-in?"

Venkman smiled down at little Oscar, noting the symbols painted on the child's body. "Hey, sailor, I think that tattoos are a little much, don't you?"

He picked up the child and hugged him.

Dana smiled at them both. "I think he likes you. I think I do too."

Venkman winked at her. "Finally came to your senses, huh?"

Across the room, Spengler, Winston, and Stantz helped the slimed Janosz to his feet. The wiry artist shook his head. "What happened?"

"Sir," Stantz intoned, "you've had a violent, prolonged, transformative psychic episode. But it's over now. Want a coffee?"

Janosz shook Ray's hand sincerely. "That's very kind of you."

Spengler examined the artist quickly. "He's fine, Ray. Physically intact, psychomagnetherically neutral."

Janosz blinked. "Is that good?"

"It's where you want to be." Winston smiled.

Janosz, the Ghostbusters, and Dana, with Oscar, walked out of the studio, passing by what had been the portrait of Vigo. The original scene, painted on the old canvas, now shone through clearly. It was a beautiful painting in the high Renaissance style depicting four archangels hovering protectively over a cherubic baby. One held a harp. One held an olive branch. The third, a book. The last, a sword.

"Late Renaissance, I think," Spengler noted. "Caravaggio or Brunelleschi."

Winston stared at the painting. "There's something very familiar about that."

He shrugged and left the room with his comrades.

A full moon shone down on the painting.

The faces of the four angels bore an uncanny resemblance to those of Venkman, Stantz, Spengler, and Winston.

The Ghostbusters exited the de-slimed museum

and were greeted with cheers from the massive crowd. Venkman pointed to Dana and her baby. The crowd spontaneously broke out into "Auld Lang Syne."

Someone handed Stantz a bottle of champagne. He held it up for the crowd's approval.

At that point a city bus pulled up in front of the museum. Louis skittered out, in full uniform lugging the oversize proton pack. He turned back to the smiling Slimer in the driver's seat.

"Okay, so Monday night we'll get something to eat and maybe go bowling? Can you bowl with those little arms?"

Slimer grunted and slobbered a reply, flexing his rubber-band biceps.

"Okay." Louis nodded. "I have to go save Dana. I'll see you later."

Slimer howled and sent the bus zigzagging off. Louis struggled through the celebrating crowd and stumbled up to the Ghostbusters.

"Am I too late?" he whined.

Stantz smiled at the diminutive fellow. "No, Louis. You're right on time."

Stantz popped the cork on the champagne bottle and handed it to Louis as the crowd continued to sing.

THE DREAM TEAM

A novel by ELLIS WEINER
based on the screenplay by
JON CONNOLLY and DAVID LOUCKA

Meet The Dream Team . . . Henry's got a doctor fixation . . .
Billy likes to put his fists through walls . . . Albert thinks he's a
baseball manager . . . and Jack's an adman whose last campaign
sent him over the edge.

If they sound a little crazy . . . well, they are. In fact, they're
certified and committed. They live in a hospital somewhere in
New Jersey, and they're about to be escorted to a Yankees game.
Just a nice, safe, little field trip – until their doctor gets mugged in
a Times Square alley. Now, these four unlikely heroes find themselves alone in the streets of New York City – the easiest place in
the world for a crazy person to get lost in a crowd.

Can four mental patients from New Jersey find happiness in the
Big Apple? Well, at least they can have one hell of a good time
trying . . .

0 552 13572 0

A SELECTED LIST OF FILM TIE-INS
AVAILABLE FROM CORGI BOOKS

THE PRICES SHOWN BELOW WERE CORRECT AT THE TIME OF
GOING TO PRESS. HOWEVER TRANSWORLD PUBLISHERS RESERVE
THE RIGHT TO SHOW NEW RETAIL PRICES ON COVERS WHICH MAY
DIFFER FROM THOSE PREVIOUSLY ADVERTISED IN THE TEXT OR
ELSEWHERE.

☐ 12569 5	The Fourth Protocol		*Frederick Forsyth*	£3.95
☐ 12774 4	Back To The Future		*George Gipe*	£2.50
☐ 13490 2	Patty Hearst	*Patricia Campbell Hearst with Alvin Moscow*		£3.99
☐ 86232 9	Ghostbusters II		*B. B. Hiller*	£2.50
☐ 10645 3	Evita		*Mary Main*	£3.99
☐ 13243 8	Robocop		*Ed Naha*	£2.50
☐ 13276 4	The Secret of My Success		*Martin Owens*	£2.50
☐ 13485 6	Red Heat		*Robert Tine*	£2.50
☐ 13570 4	Rooftops		*Robert Tine*	£2.50
☐ 13572 0	The Dream Team		*Ellis Weiner*	£2.99

All Corgi/Bantam Books are available at your bookshop or newsagent, or can
be ordered from the following address:
Corgi/Bantam Books,
Cash Sales Department,
P.O. Box 11, Falmouth, Cornwall TR10 9EN

Please send a cheque or postal order (no currency) and allow 60p for postage
and packing for the first book plus 25p for the second book and 15p for each
additional book ordered up to a maximum charge of £1.90 in UK.

B.F.P.O. customers please allow 60p for the first book, 25p for the second book plus
15p per copy for the next 7 books, thereafter 9p per book.

Overseas customers, including Eire, please allow £1.25 for postage and packing
for the first book, 75p for the second book, and 28p for each subsequent title
ordered.

NAME (Block Letters) ....

ADDRESS ....

....